Alice and Me

Alice and Me

A NOVEL BY
WILLIAM JUDSON

ARTHUR FIELDS BOOKS, INC. | NEW YORK

Published simultaneously in Canada
by Clarke, Irwin & Company Limited,
Toronto and Vancouver
SBN: 0-525-630007
Library of Congress Catalog Card Number: 72-94675

For my dear friend Morris Elowitz,
Attorney at Law, who lived
part of the story.

Alice and Me

ONE

On my seventieth birthday I woke up with a hangover, a hard-on, and sixteen dollars cash money in the whole world. That was out in Springfield, Kansas, which is my home town, and where I lived all my life except for two trips to Alaska, which I'll get around to when the fancy strikes me.

So this here's the big city?

Well, if you'll pardon me for saying so, you can have it. But I do thank you for listening to an old man ramble on. I'm Fred Frederickson. And I want to tell you about Alice and me. If you ain't got nothing better to do, why don't you just put your feet up and sit for a spell?

Like I said, there I was, busted flat on my ass and no place to go. A sorry pass for a man, right square on his birthday. It ain't no fun being alone on your birthday, particularly when you got a hard-on. You see, my wife died a good spell back, whereupon my three ungrateful

daughters ran out on me with her insurance money—
they were Pauline, Patience, and Pamela, and my
advice is to steer clear of them if you get the chance.
That was a good twenty years ago, but there still ain't
a night I don't fall down on my knees and pray to Al-
mighty God that those three don't change their minds
and come back.

Well, I breathed me such a hearty sigh of relief that
the three little bitches was gone that I managed to con-
vince the United States Navy that I was pretty healthy,
and what with a little lying about my age (I told that
there doctor I was thirty-two, and he believed me) I got
me a commission in the Seabees and went up to Alaska
in command of a heavy equipment battalion. Now, that
was in the summer of 1943. I went up that way once before, in 1921, when I wasn't much more than a tad. I
had notions of stumbling over piles of gold under them
northern lights, but all I fell over was my own clumsy
feet and had to sell my grandfather's 30-30 Winches-
ter '73, which near to busted my heart.

The old man left me that rifle in his will, and I was
real attached to it. Well, I got back to Springfield and
settled down to getting married and minding my own
business, which was the John Deere farm equipment
agency my father left me one spring morning when he
cranked a combine-harvester that was already in gear.

The years went by without nothing special happening. I did me a lot of fishing and some hunting with
my little .22 Savage. It didn't have much range, and the
hitting power of that tiny 40-grain bullet wasn't nothing to brag about, but I got my white-tailed deer every

year by hitting him smack between the eyes, and that way you don't ruin any meat either, like them heavy-caliber rifle boys do, jellying a whole front leg with their artillery when they miss the boiler factory, which is what we call the heart and lung target area. I got me plenty of quail and partridge with the same little gun, and most days I brought home ten birds for the ten shells I took out. Once in a while I missed, but when I did, I was beholden to line up the next shot so I got two birds with the same bullet.

Up there in Alaska, though, I found out that my .22 just wasn't gun enough for them moose and caribou and black bear. My first hunt was enough to make a preacher cuss. I hit a twelve-hundred-pound bull moose right between the eyes, and that horny bastard just laughed at me. I put three more .22 slugs in his chest cavity and sat down to wait while old Mr. Moose, he charged off into the stand of dark green spruce pines. Well, finally he stiffened up and lay down to die from internal bleeding, but we had to hack the meat up with an axe and pack it out almost a mile to our canoe, Indian Pete and me, and every step of the way I cussed that little .22 Savage.

Next day, I went down to Fairbanks and spent three hundred dollars on guns and ammunition. I picked me up a sporterized Springfield '03 and a couple of boxes of 30.06 slugs for it. The rifle had a four-power Weaver telescopic sight, which I wanted taken off. I never held much with glass sights. It always seemed to me they was going out of whack just when you needed them. But the salesman argued me out of it. He showed me the ballistic tables, and I could see plain that with a bullet that didn't drop more than five or six inches at three hundred yards, them iron sights was just too coarse for tight patterns. That salesman didn't believe me when I told him I was used to stalking my game up close, around thirty paces or so, and finally, mostly to avoid an argument, I let the scope stay.

I won't wear you down with the ins and out of those three years I spent up there in the North Country, building airfields and hunting. As a matter of fact, I'm pretty sure you don't even want to hear it.

I've learned one thing since I been here in New York City. You city fellers just can't understand the way hunting tests a man to the limit. You ain't willing to face up to sudden death; you just won't believe it's natural for man to be a hunter. You're scared of guns because you can't use them yourself and you're positive that if anybody else gets his hands on one, he'll aim it at you.

But it seems kind of horseshit to me that the very same city feller who squeezes up his lips and bad-mouths me for "killing those defenseless animals" will rip apart his fellow man, tear him to shreds, all in the name of "business." Of course, the city's *his* territory, and he hunts it his own way. But I tell you true, a lot of the stuff you city people get away with every day would get you shot in the head real fast if you lived out in the woods.

Anyway, I won't bore you with all the stories I could tell about some of the best hunting a man ever got in.

But I was real proud of my final total, so I'll put it down for you. In them three years, I got:

9 moose
14 caribou
6 black bear
2 polar bear
7 walrus (they was food for the Eskimo workers)
Geese, duck, partridge, varying hare and other small
  game too numerous to mention.
And one Esquimau.

Or, if you spell it this way, Eskimo. This one was blessed with a name and a human face, but if you want the truth, he was worse than any wild animal I ever tracked. He had raped and murdered a little girl from a neighboring village, and maybe that in itself was understandable, because the Eskimo, like our own American Indian, he's never been able to square his old habits and inclinations with the effects of the white man's whiskey. And that would have been taken into account at his trial. But there wasn't any trial, because he never reached Fairbanks. He was in the custody of a couple of Shore Policemen, and on the way down a blizzard hit them. The jeep was snowbound, and them S.P.'s probably took off his handcuffs to give him a better chance to come out alive. He must have jumped them and hit them with a chunk of ice, anyway that's what we figured, but we couldn't be sure, because there wasn't enough left of them two boys to tell *how* he killed them. That storm, it lasted for nine days, and in that time, Mr. Eskimo, he et good. We didn't find nothing but burned bones and those boys' two heads, and that

wasn't the worst, either. There was one leg bone missing, because old Mr. Eskimo, he'd taken along some
emergency rations for the trail.

Well, as you might know, The Law didn't catch him.
How could they? He knew them woods better than any
white man. But, just luck, I was out hunting a couple of
weeks later, and I caught me a glimpse of him between
the trees, only a quick flash.

Most of the time a hunter's got plenty of time to
stalk his quarry, plan his aim, and place his shots. But
once in a while the game'll flush suddenly and leap
across a road or a firebreak. That gives you just frac-
tions of a second to pull up and fire—or choose *not* to
fire. There ain't no time for thought; it's plain reflex.
Does that deer have horns? If so, lead him with the
cross hairs, just above and in front of the outstretched
nose, squeeze the trigger, and go over to finish off the
thrashing, twitching body on the ground. If there ain't
no horns, it's a doe, don't shoot. And make up your
mind, mister, in less time than it takes to blink an eye.

That's just the way it was when I come on the Eskimo. I got me one quick glimpse of his head and
shoulders as he passed between two balsam trees. But
that was long enough to tell he was an Eskimo, and he
had on blue navy clothes and a pea jacket, and he was
carrying an issue carbine.

What happened next was hunter's reflex. I clicked off
the safety, threw the 30.06 to my shoulder, centered the
scope's cross hairs on the dark blob of his chest, and
squeezed off a round. Mixed up with the muzzle blast,
I heard the sharp slap of the bullet striking flesh. I

ducked down behind a windfall, ejected the empty, rammed a fresh shell into the chamber, and waited.

For a long time there wasn't any sound but the sigh of the wind through the snow-drooped balsam trees. Then, from far down the trail, I heard him give out a low, pulsating moan, followed by a couple of rasping snorts, just like an angry buck blowing. I waited. After a while there came a series of crunching, thrashing noises, like something pawing frantically at the snow.

I didn't move. The snow cover was crusty enough that I didn't have to worry about anybody sneaking up on me. And I was sure I'd hit him with the 150-grain soft-nosed bullet. At that range, it would have torn through bone and muscle with around 2500 foot-pounds of energy. He wouldn't be going nowhere.

When the forest had been quiet for a good ten minutes, I made a circle and sneaked up on him from the rear. It wasn't necessary. He'd somehow managed to crawl four or five feet off the trail, leaving great lumps of blood and viscera in his path, and had died face down in the snow. I rolled him over to check where the bullet had hit. It was lower than I had wanted. Instead of smashing through the heart, the slug unzipped his paunch like a sharp knife and, gut-shot, he had lived long enough to make the few sounds I'd heard. I cussed that telescopic sight; it must have gotten knocked out of line and was shooting low.

As you'd imagine, dragging the body back to my jeep was a messy business. The slug had opened Mr. Eskimo's belly from crotch to rib cage. I buttoned his pea jacket up tight, but there was still bits of Eskimo strewn along a two-hundred-yard drag track through the deep snow. It was uphill, and hard going, and all the way I kept thinking of that Polack hunting joke. There was these two Polacks out deer hunting, and one Polack mistook the other for a buck and shot him. Well, he hightailed it out of there and got his buddy to the hospital, but it wasn't any use. The doctor come out of the operating room shaking his head and said, "Sorry, I couldn't save him. The bullet wound wasn't bad—but why did you have to gut him out?"

Didn't figure you'd laugh. I never met a city feller yet who thought that joke was funny. But your hunter, he laughs his head off. Because he understands that the first thing any hunter does, even before he sits down, is dress out his kill. All you got to do is let it go once and let your animal bloat, and then have to cut him open and smell the rising, sickening odor from gas-swole guts, and you won't hesitate the next time to get out the knife, and that's why that joke is funny. Except some of you don't get the point.

Mr. Eskimo, legally at least, was a man, so instead of doing the right and natural thing, I gave myself the extra work of dragging thirty pounds of useless guts all the way to my jeep. It wasn't until later that it dawned on me, I could have left him where he fell. Maybe the wolves might of eaten most of him before I got back with The Law, but that wouldn't have mattered anyway. As it was, they just dumped him in an unmarked grave after we had a meeting in the mayor's office, where I refused the $500 reward on his head. I do not shoot man nor beast for profit.

One thing always bothered me. After I got old Mr.

Eskimo the way he deserved, people kind of shied away from me up there, as if I was something strange. How do you figure that? All I done was what was right and called for, and they even offered me a reward, but afterward they all seemed a little scared of me.

Well, after the war, I went back to Kansas, and like you'd figure, it seemed awful tame and citified. But I made the best of things, and hunted every year in Wyoming for antelope and big-horn sheep. Then, ten years ago, when I was sixty, I sold out the John Deere agency and settled down to enjoying myself hunting and fishing and waiting for that Grim Reaper to sneak up and tap me on the shoulder. But somewhere along the way, I lost myself. You see, to the folks around me, my life was ended; I was just another old man. But I couldn't see things that way. So I guess I set out to drink as much booze and screw as many women as any man in Kansas, just to prove I could do it. And I could, too.

But I kind of miscalculated. It seems like my liver must be made of shoe leather, so in spite of the way I whooped things up, my bank account give out before *I* did, and when I was seventy, I was broke.

Never having been poor before, it didn't worry me too much, but I had to leave Kansas because it started my friends to stewing about me, and I could see in their eyes they was about to start offering me little "loans" and a place to sleep, and naturally I couldn't permit that kind of nonsense. So I decided to go to Wyoming and build me a little hunting camp. I got on the highway, stuck out my thumb, and crawled into the first truck that stopped.

Outliving my money was bad luck. Could have hap-

pened to anybody. But getting lost on a goddamned su-
perhighway was plain stupidity, and all my fault. I got
a compass, carried it all my life. And I'm ashamed to
say that when I got out on that highway, I never even
took the goddamned thing from my pocket, and I must
have got myself turned around on one of them clover-
leafs. You know, if you turn left on one of them it
makes a circle and you end up heading *right*. When I
did notice I was headed the wrong direction I was just
too damned stubborn to turn around, and that's how I
ended up here in New York City instead of Wyoming.
God's truth, and I ain't a bit proud of myself. Of course,
I didn't have to stay, but then I met Alice and didn't
want to leave just yet. So I settled down here and
learned how to hate city style, which is the worst style
there is.

Now, if you're ready, I'll tell you about Alice and
me, but first let's have a drink.

TWO

Alice.

When I first saw her over there by the fountain, you can understand how it wasn't too surprising that I took her for a boy. She went six feet easy, and her hair was cut short, and she wore blue jeans and an old field jacket with a Third Armored Division patch on the shoulder and dark shadows on the sleeves where sergeant's chevrons used to be.

"Hey, buddy," I yelled. "How do I get out of this goddamned place?"

We had driven through a tunnel, the trucker and me, and I asked him to put me down near the first tree we saw. It turned out to be Washington Square in that crazy nest of old buildings they call Greenwich Village. It was late afternoon, and the wind was cold and it tumbled dirty newspapers into the dried-up fountain. All around the square the gray, ugly buildings huddled like heaps of slag from a strip mine. No siree, I decided, this place ain't for me; I want to head for the tall timber and the high country.

When I yelled, she turned around, and I saw then that she was a girl.

"Shove off, grandpa," she said.

"Whoops," I said. "Sorry, mister, I didn't know you was a girl."

"Get lost."

"That's my problem," I told her. "I'm *already* lost."

We was standing in the middle of one of them winding paths, squared off toward each other like two stray dogs, and it was so funny that I had to laugh out loud. The girl tightened her lips and I thought she was going to swing on me, and I held up both hands.

"I give up, lady. I ain't laughing at you, believe me. It's just that I been in the piney woods most of my life, and now here I am, lost right in the middle of a goddamned *city*."

She almost smiled then. Almost, but not quite. It was a long time before I ever saw a real smile on those lips.

"Are you really lost, old-timer?"

"Lost! Lady, I'm so turned around I couldn't find my ass with both hands. I'm so twisted up that you couldn't straighten me out with a magnet and twenty pounds of angle irons. I'm——"

"Ho!" she said, waving me down. "Whoa! Enough! I got the idea. Now, where is it you want to go?"

"Laramie, Wyoming'll do fine."

She shook her head. "I'm afraid that's a little out of my territory."

"If you don't mind me asking, where *is* your territory? What kind of outfit is that you're wearing, anyway?" I looked her up and down, making sure she saw me do it. "What are you anyway, one of those hippies?"

She didn't answer at first, then she shook her head slowly. "No . . . I'm just short of money for things like clothes."

"Well, I'm busted too," I said. "But my clothes are neat. I ain't dirty. And I don't smell."

"Could be," she told me. "But at least, *I'm* not lost."

I let out a whoop you could have heard all the way to Fairbanks. "You got me," I said. "I set myself up in line for that one and you slipped it to me real good. Lady, I admire your spirit. What the hell are you doing loafing around this scrawny patch of woods and concrete they call a park? Underneath that scarecrow's outfit I bet there's a good chunk of woman. Why ain't you housed up somewhere with a man?"

"You old coot," she said, almost smiling again, "You talk pretty dirty for a wreck with one foot in the grave. Do you get your kicks mouthing off about what you can't do any more yourself?"

"Hoo! Don't get that idea," I said. "I may be seventy years old, but any time you think I can't cut the mustard, you just lean over a little. Next thing you know, you're liable to be kicking your heels in midair."

Her face changed and she turned away. "See you around."

I hurried to draw her back. "Now, don't get your innards in an uproar. I never meant to talk dirty to you, and if you think I was, why I'm sorry. I say things straight out, the way they come to me, and sometimes they come out a little rough. But I meant no offense. Just the opposite. I was trying to pass you a compliment."

She looked down at her shoes. "Thank you. I guess I'm not used to compliments much anymore." She looked around the park. It was almost dark. "Listen, I can take you down to Canal Street where you go through the Holland Tunnel for New Jersey. But I don't know if you'd get a ride now. They don't pick people up after dark, not even when you're a girl."

I studied her. I hadn't been lying to her. She *was* a handsome chunk of woman, if only she'd wash her face and put on some proper clothes. "You sound like you've been down that route yourself."

She nodded. "Once in a while I hitch out to the country. In the summer you can go to one of the state parks and if you don't cause any trouble you can sit down in the woods and look at the running water. Once I even saw a deer. At least, I think it was a deer. It was all brown and there were horns on its head."

I felt so sorry for her right then that I totally forgot about my own problem of getting out to Wyoming and setting up a camp before the snow flew. It just seemed so goddamned *miserable* that a body would have to hitchhike way the hell and gone out to some state park just to see a stream—and even when she saw a deer, it was so new and strange that she didn't know what she was watching. Now, I have always been used to being alone, and far from bothering me, it has been more pleasure than not. But this big girl in her dirty jeans and army jacket didn't like being alone. It worked on her, like the wind works on loose house shingles, nibbling and probing until it gets a good hold and then rips them away to reveal the soft, unprotected wood beneath. Something had been ripping at this girl. You could see the bare spots.

"That was most likely a deer," I said. "That is, if it didn't give milk and say 'moo.' Did it give you a good feeling, watching it?"

"Oh, yes."

"Then that was a deer for sure. There ain't nothing that'll give a body more pleasure than watching a deer in the woods. I think I'd as soon watch a deer as shoot one."

She looked at me sharply. "You don't *shoot* them!"

I grinned. "One or two, in my day."

"That's awful!"

Before I could answer, two boys appeared. They were padding along on the grass, walking real careful without making any noise. There was something *mean* about the way they moved, like they were ashamed of letting anyone see them. They come right up to me and one stood close in front of me while the other one started to tippytoe around behind my back.

"Hey, man," said the one in front, "spare a cigarette?" His hair was all fluffed up in a blond Afro, and his teeth smelled like dog shit.

I took a step back so I could see the other one from the corner of my eyes. He had been doing something with his hands, and they dropped suddenly to his sides as I looked at him.

"Never smoke cigarettes," I said. "Please don't crowd me so close, boy."

"Don't jive us, man," whined the other one, still circling to get behind me. He must have been a Mexican, or maybe one of them Puerto Ricans. His skin was sallow, and his hair was slicked down with oil.

The girl stepped toward us. "Bug off," she told the boys. "Leave him alone."

"Keep out of this," said the one in front. He turned his stinking breath on me again. "Look, grandpa, loosen up, slip us the price of a pack of butts. Just a buck."

I sensed movement behind me. This was bad. They wouldn't settle for a dollar. They would take it all, and whether or not they kicked the shit out of me afterward depended on how happy they were with their haul. Lousy, sneaking punks—two- or four-legged, they are always the same. Whining pet house dogs, running in packs through the woods, they'll drag down a pregnant doe and rip the living fawns from her guts and then go home, tail between their legs, and grovel for table scraps. And there ain't no reasoning with them.

I made my voice go all old and shaky. "Please, I'm an old man. Please don't hurt me."

Saying "please" to their sort is like asking them to slap you around. The girl shouted a warning, but I already knew that the punk behind me was grabbing for my wrists while the one in front threw a clumsy punch at my belly. I dove forward, kicking back with my right heel. It connected with something soft and the one behind me shrieked like a pig being stuck. I got both hands around the other one's shoulders and butted him in the gut with my head. He grunted and I kicked him in the ankle and he fell down and I put my shoe on his throat.

"Boy," I said quietly, "I think I will break your no-good neck."

His eyes popped up at me, and he started gabbling something so fast that I couldn't tell what he was saying. I let him sweat and plead while I looked over to see what had happened to the other one. He was rolling over and over on the grass grabbing at his nuts and howling like a dog with turpentine up its ass.

Distantly, I heard the warbling moan of a siren. The girl grabbed at my shoulder.

"Fuzz!" she yelled. "Come on!"

"The Law? Good. I can't wait to turn these punks over to them."

"No, no, no!" she said frantically. "You don't understand! This is *New York*! They'll want to know who you are, and where you live, and where you work. You're on the bum, you'll wind up in more trouble than they will."

I looked down at them. The one was still barking like a dog and the other was lying dead still under my boot, his eyes rolling like white grapes.

"That don't hardly seem right," I said. "Do you mean these turds might get off after what they tried to do?"

"Of *course* they'll get off," she said impatiently. "But *you* won't. Listen, are you coming?"

"Hold your horses, lady," I said. "Just let me consider what to do."

I bent down toward the one under my foot. He closed his eyes and started to cry. "What *are* you?" I asked. "You're too big for a boy and too miserable for a man. I'd say you was a rat except you ain't got four legs.

You ain't even a chicken, because you don't wear feathers, although that mess on your head could fool a body."

He found his voice. "Please, Mister, don't hurt me. We didn't mean nothing."

I squoze his windpipe off with my foot. "Nope," I said. "You didn't mean nothing, except to beat up on an old man and take his money and anything else that suited your fancy. Boy, I don't like your looks much. I think I'll do the world a favor and fix you up so *nobody'll* like them, ever again."

Before he could move, I shifted my foot and put the full weight of my body square on top of his nose and twisted my hobnailed boot. He gave a gurgling shriek and fainted. Bright red blood spilled down over both his cheeks. The big girl gasped and started to pull away, but I took her arm and walked her toward the park fence. On the way, I gave the second boy another jab behind the ear with my boot and he fell face down and got quiet.

Frightened, the girl said, "My God, you're crazy. You may have killed them."

"Not hardly. But they won't be too chipper for a spell anyway, which is only fair considering what they had in mind for me."

Two blue-uniformed policemen tore into the park just as we left it. I put on my old man's voice and quavered, "Praise God you came, Officers. Those two boys like to killed each other, fighting over them funny-looking cigarettes they was smoking."

The policemen didn't even bother to thank me, just

ran off toward the crowd that was already gathering curiously under the leaf-bare trees.

We got ourselves a table in one of them fancy places that call themselves coffee houses and I ordered two cups of regular American, black. They was the cheapest listed on the big menu painted on the wall and they were still forty cents each.

"This place is expensive," said the girl. "If you only wanted coffee, we could have gone to Rikers or——"

"Hush up," I said. "I wanted a place where we could set a spell and visit. Most counter places are always too anxious for you to finish up and move on the minute your cup gets low."

We sat there and listened to the funny longhair music from the hi-fi until the coffee came. I took out a pint of Old Crow and offered it to the girl. She shuddered and shook her head. I sweetened mine real good and took a swig. It was passable. I made a little toast toward the girl.

"Here's your good health, ma'am," I said. "I want to tell you, I sure did admire the way you stood up for me against them two in the park. Why, I do believe you'd a swung on them yourself if I hadn't beat you to it."

"Mister," she said, holding her cup in two hands to try and keep it from slopping over, and failing because of the way she was trembling, "you scare me. That's the only reason I'm sitting here with you. If I weren't so scared, I'd be putting distance between us this very minute."

"I sure am sorry you feel that way," I said. "If what

you say is so, why don't you just get up and be on your way? I'll finish my coffee and then I'll get packing for Laramie."

She put the cup down. "You won't follow me?"

"What would I do that for? Thank you for your kindness, ma'am, and good luck to you."

She got up fast and started for the door. Then she turned and said, "Good luck to you too," and left.

Well. I knew I was slipping, but that was the first live one I'd let get away since Jasper was a pup. And a roaring shame, too, if she was anywhere near the chunk of female I thought she was. I don't go much for short hair on women, but it would have grown out.

You win a few and lose a few. It was dark outside, now. Pretty soon I would have to find that there Canal Street and get started for Wyoming. But there wasn't any big hurry. I sweetened her coffee with bourbon and drank it too.

Someone was standing at my elbow. Without looking up, I said, "I thought you were on your way."

The big girl said, "I really thought you were going to follow me."

I looked up at her. "Why?"

"I don't know. Money, maybe. But I don't have any."

"I never took money from a woman one day in my life. And if I was to start, it wouldn't be with you, big woman."

"I don't have *anything* you'd want," she said.

"You surely *do* have something I'd want," I said. "But I wouldn't creep after you to get it."

There was a touch of smile on her lips as she sat down. "You're all brag."

"That just may be. Try me."

She looked away. "It was terrifying," she said. "The way you handled those two. Like some kind of terrible machine. I was afraid you'd kill them." She covered her breasts with both arms. "I keep getting goosebumps, just thinking about it."

"It ain't nothing special, killing a feller when he deserves it."

"No one deserves it."

"I knew one that did. An Eskimo feller, up in Alaska, during the war."

I told her about him, and she shuddered and said, "He was sick. Insane."

"So what if he was? He killed and et them two boys as slick and smart as you please, didn't he?"

"Please," she said. "I don't like to hear of violence."

"Neither do I. But sometimes you got to face it."

"Don't," she said. "It's. . . . Look, if you're hungry, well, it isn't much, but if you want to come over to my place, I can at least feed you supper before you try to hitchhike all the way to Wyoming."

"Are you sure it won't put you out?"

"I wouldn't have offered if it was too much trouble."

"In that case, ma'am, I'm much obliged."

We stood up. She said, "My name is Alice. Alice Gordon."

"Fred."

"Fred what?"

"Fred Frederickson. Fred all the way."

THREE

Alice was right. Her place wasn't much. The building might have been red brick once upon a time, but it was greasy gray now from a century of soot and truck exhausts. The hallway inside wasn't any better; the front door hung from its hinges and whoever had kicked it down must have used the space under the stairs for a urinal.

"What have they been doing?" I asked. "Pissing in the hall?"

Alice looked around as if she were seeing the hallway for the first time. "We can't keep that outside door closed. They just break it down. So there's no point in cleaning the hall. The addicts always get in and mess it right up again."

"Why don't you lay for them and mess up a few addicts?"

"What good would that do? There'd just be others along tomorrow night. You can't keep them out."

I didn't say anything else as we climbed up the two flights of stairs, but I was sore tempted to turn right around and head for Wyoming.

Alice only had what you'd call a room and a half. The biggest part, the "room," was sort of a living room with a sofa and some chairs and a table. The "half" was a ratty little kitchenette that looked like it had been taken out of one of those pickup truck camper units. But everything was clean, and she'd tried to cheer the place up with pictures and plastic flowers. They didn't succeed. It only looked lonely and forlorn.

She had to undo three locks to let us in. One was a Yale padlock on a hasp. The other two went through the door, and when we got inside I saw that one was connected to a long iron bar that poked down into a hole in the floor.

"Afraid of your neighbors?" I asked.

"You'd be afraid, too, if you'd been broken into as often as I have. Before I put on this police lock, they hit me three weeks in a row. That's why I don't have a TV set, or even a radio. They took everything that wasn't nailed down."

"Well, that little Yale padlock outside won't do you much good. I could break that off with the end of a beer bottle."

"I know. But if someone pries it off, at least I'll know they're inside before I walk in myself. Sally, she's a girl who lived upstairs, she walked in on a couple of addicts ransacking her place. They grabbed her before she could get away."

"What happened?"

Alice turned her hands up helplessly. "She died. Maybe they didn't mean to kill her, but they did anyway. They hung her in the closet with a gag in her mouth, like an old overcoat. She choked."

"Jesus H. Christ!" I said "How in hell can you live here, girl?"

"It's all I can afford." She gestured around the tiny apartment. "Seventy bucks a month. I can pay next month's rent because I've still got three weeks of unemployment coming. After that, I just don't know."

"Unemployment? What's a healthy girl like you doing taking charity anway?"

"Charity my ass!" she flared. "I've paid my share and then some into the unemployment insurance fund. Some of the biggest movie stars in Hollywood go down and collect when they're between films. Why shouldn't I? But anyway, it isn't much, and that's the reason I live in this place."

"Settle down, big woman," I said. "Besides, I didn't mean why you live *here*. I meant this lousy city. I can't hardly wait to put it all behind me."

She stripped off her field jacket and threw it on the sofa. "Well, don't let *me* slow you down, old-timer. There's the door, and Canal Street is due south."

I headed for the door. "Many thanks for the directions, ma'am."

I was fumbling with the bar of the police lock when she caught up with me and pulled at my arm. "Don't be like that, grandpa."

"My name is Fred, I ain't your grandpa, and it only takes one invitation to get me moving."

She squeezed her big body between me and the door. "I'm *un*inviting, all right? Just please don't bug me about this place. I don't like it very much, but it's the only game in town."

I let her lead me back to the sofa. "You talk like a gambler. You ever play cards?"

"Sometimes."

"How about a game of strip poker?"

"You're an old fraud."

"Try me and see."

She studied my face, decided I wasn't joking, and laughed. "Maybe later. Do you want to wash up?"

"If it ain't too much trouble."

"It's through the kitchen. Don't you have a suitcase somewhere?"

I patted the pockets of my jacket. "Got everything I need right here. Razor, soap, washrag."

"Don't you have any other clothes?"

"I'm wearing two shirts. When I light somewhere, I wash one and wear the other."

"What about underwear?"

"Never bother with it. Slows me down."

She gave an elaborate, much-exaggerated sigh. "Go on, grandpa, wash your face."

"Can I use your bathtub?"

"It's a shower."

"Even better. Want to wash my back?"

She shoved me toward the kitchen. "Get in there, you old goat, before I lose my patience."

I opened the bathroom door, turned back to her. "You know, lady, you wouldn't melt if you'd try a little soap and water yourself."

She had extra towels, so I used one of them instead of the scrap of flannel cloth I carry, and I shaved and scrubbed my teeth with soap and the corner of my washcloth. Then I took a quick shower, and while I was in there, I rinsed out the inner shirt I'd been wearing and hung it over the shower rail to dry. I did the same for the socks I'd been wearing, dried off and put on the spares from my coat pocket, the same old pants and the outside shirt.

When I went back into the living room, her back was toward me. I stood behind her.

"All spick and span," I said.

She didn't answer. I went around the sofa and she twisted her head in the opposite direction. She was crying.

"Hey," I said. "Hey."

"Get out of here."

"Listen," I said, "I didn't mean to upset you."

"I thought it only took one invitation to send you on your way."

She twisted and turned, but I still captured one of her hands in mine and sat down beside her, holding it. "I only said what I did because I like you. If I didn't like you, you could dip yourself in cowshit like an Indian squaw for all I'd care."

"You said I'm dirty."

"Well, goddamn it, you *are* dirty."

"Get the hell out of here."

"Listen to me first, big woman."

"I'm not interested."

I looked around. "You got this place fixed up nice, there's curtains on the windows and everything. So why do you walk around with an inch of soot on your face?"

"That's my business."

"Maybe. But let me tell you something I've noticed about animals. When they're running free, the way nature intended, they keep themselves clean and neat as a pin. But you put too much pressure on them, fence them in, make too much noise that they don't understand, and right away they get short-tempered, they get mean—and most of all, they get *dirty*.

"Who the hell cares?"

"You can call it a nervous breakdown, call it anything you please, it's still the first step on the way to breakfast with the buzzards."

"Where'd you learn all the big words, grandpa?"

I leaned over and patted her on the knee. "I give you fair warning, Alice, the very next time you call me grandpa, I am going to feel obliged to put you over my knee and give you a few whacks where your pants is tightest."

"Try it."

I moved toward her and she drew back, both fists clenched. Her teeth were almost bared. I laughed. "Now, that's more like it. Fight back, Alice. Don't let the bastards grind you down."

"Up yours, grand—I mean, Fred."

"You're learning. Tell you what I'm going to do, big woman. You try out that there soap and water and see how you like it, and meanwhile I'll rustle up something to eat. Fair?"

She stared at me. "What gives you the right to interfere with the way I live?"

"Because I took a liking to you, lady. Do I need a license for that?"

Her frown softened, and she looked like she was ready to cry again. "No. . . ."

"Now, you go crawl in that shower."

"Listen, Fred," she said, "I don't want you getting any ideas. I may be a little mixed up, but I haven't been working the streets or——"

"Never thought you were," I said. "Dirty as you are, you'd of had to pay *them*."

"Oh!" she yelled. "Goddamn you, Fred Frederickson!"

"The shower's waiting, girl."

She must have been faking her anger, for it went away as quick as it came. "All right, Fred," she said. Then, at the bathroom door: "Do you want to wash *my* back?"

I made a grab at her. "You're a shameless woman."

She laughed and slammed the door. Pretty soon I heard water running.

While she got clean and I rustled up something to eat, I talked to her through the door. "You know, Alice, like I was saying about how animals get pushed too far and just give up? Now old Mr. Eskimo I told you about, he was a genuine case of what I meant. It didn't matter that he only heard a jeep a couple of times a day, and maybe had to go to work three days a week. It was still too much for him to handle. He went off his rocker."

Alice came out with a blue robe wrapped around her. She had a towel turbaned on her head. She looked all glowing and warm, and I couldn't help but get a little stirred up. "You look real pretty now," I told her.

She pulled the robe tightly around her and changed the subject back to old Mr. Eskimo. "But why did you have to *kill* him?"

"Lady, it was easy. I never had bad dream number one about it. I figure there's me and mine, and then there's the rest of them. He was one of them, not one of *us*. You stop and think about it, he wasn't even *real*. Not to me. Oh, he murdered that little girl all right, and them navy boys who was only doing their jobs, but that ain't why I killed him, Alice."

Softly, she asked, "Then why did you?"

"Because if I saw him, he might of seen *me* too. No sirree, I wasn't going to give that Eskimo gentleman no chance to come after me because he was afraid I might turn him in."

"But that's just what you *should* have done, reported him to the law."

"Whose law? The law that stood beside us in that park a while ago and kept those two punks from beating up on me? The law that stood between your friend Sally upstairs and those addicts? The law that would have kept that crazy Eskimo from plugging me and maybe roasting me up for breakfast?"

"But you can't go around *killing* people!"

"I don't go looking for them, Alice. They come and found me. But think on this: when you let them get away, they're liable to double back and kill *you*. I don't see no point in giving them the chance."

Shuddering, she said, "I know. I saw. The way you kicked that poor boy in the head. . . ."

"Lady," I said, my voice hard, "that 'poor boy' wanted nothing better than to cut my throat. I just beat him to the punch. And if more people hit first, there'd be a hell of a lot less misery afterward."

"But you *can't*! You can't just take the law into your own hands."

"Who says so? The punks? The addicts? The ones who are out to get *us*! What the hell do we owe *them*?"

Alice spread her hands. The robe fell open and I got a good look at firm, pink boobies before she got herself wrapped up again. "We've got to have rules, Fred," she said, all in a rush like the words could cover up what I'd seen. "If we want to live in a civilization, we have to abide by its rules."

I nodded at the door with its triple locks. "Ain't them the same rules that say you've got to lock yourself up in here like some animal trapped in a cage? Where was your civilization when that poor girl upstairs was choking to death in her own coat closet? Why don't your civilization's rules keep them addicts from kicking down your front door and pissing on your stairs?"

"The system's not perfect," she admitted. "But we're trying. And one thing is clear, violence simply isn't the answer. If we got rid of all the guns and knives——"

"Alice, I declare I plain don't know what I'm going to do with you." I made a move toward her, and she drew back and the robe came open again. She tucked it around her, but not so fast this time. "Do you really believe that just because *you* ain't going to carry guns that *they* won't? Do you believe that when you turn the other cheek, they ain't going to bash it in with an axe? You don't really think that laying low and praying loud is going to turn aside one single punk or thief who wants what you got? Like hell, girl. You got to stand up for yourself, because nobody else in this world will. If you don't kick them first, they'll kick you. Never let them sneak around behind you. And once you get them down, give them one more kick in the head for good measure. That is, unless you want to wind up dead. That's the way things are, Alice, and that's the way they'll always be. Believe it or not, people just ain't nice."

Quietly, she said, "I hope you're not right, Fred. Because if you are, I don't know how I could go on living."

"Well, if you want to stop living, just turn your back on those bastards. They'll fix you up."

She turned away. "I'm going to get dressed now. Don't look."

"No fear. You ain't got nothing I never saw before. Get pretty, and meanwhile I'll spread out the food."

We ate, and it was good, and we drank some cheap wine Alice had in the refrigerator, and then we sat around and talked a lot without saying much. I felt like a twenty-year-old on his first date, which ain't a bad way to feel, and Alice knew, like women always do. She didn't put a stop to what was happening, so she was just asking for what come next. Oh, she made a couple of bad jokes and called me grandpa once, which gave me an excuse to tan her backside in a friendly fashion, and once we had touched each other, the rest came naturally. Halfway through the first time, she dug her nails into my back and whispered, "Not so fast. You're sweating. Your heart'll give out," and I started laughing so hard I came near to falling out of the saddle.

"Are you sure it's my *heart* you're worried might give out?" That got her to laughing too, and we had to sit up and drink some wine before we could get serious enough to start again.

Now, I don't know what kind of pictures go through your mind when you think of a seventy-year-old coot like me being with a young woman, hardly more than a girl, like Alice. If they's dirty pictures, why then I'm truly sorry for you, because there ain't nothing dirty about two people celebrating life in the best way there is.

Well, there ain't no need to spend more time on it. It happened, and it was good, and what's wrong with that?

FOUR

I'm the kind of feller who always tries to leave his campsite in better shape than it was when he came. I pick up the beer cans, rebuild the fireplace, cut wood and leave it for the next guy.

So, when Alice and me was having breakfast, I did a little nosing around to find out how I could help her.

Turned out, she was born in Akron, Ohio. She went to some little college out there and majored in drama. Five years back, she'd come to New York City with her diploma, nine hundred dollars in cash money, and a letter of introduction to the manager of one of them off-Broadway theaters.

I never was one much for playgoing, on account of they hardly never came out our way, so when Alice told me how she'd played Hedda Gabler and some Greek woman named Electra, I didn't know what the hell she was talking about. I used to go to the movies, but them ladies never turned up there. But from the way she talked, I figured Alice must have been pretty good. What went against her all the time, though, was that she was so damned *big*. There just ain't many actors around who can stand up and look tall and manly against an actress who goes nearly six feet in her stockings.

"Alice, I said, "don't you think that maybe you went in for the wrong business? You're a big woman, and most actors I seen are little shrimps. The odds were against you before you started."

She flared up and pointed out that Colleen Dewhurst is a big woman too, but with no disrespect intended, I never heard of the lady and anyway I'd make a bet that *she* wasn't no six feet tall. Alice didn't like it, but she had to agree.

Well, her nine hundred dollars was gone soon enough, and Alice went the down route, starting out at the Barbizon Hotel for Women, and spiraling all the way to the bottom, this seventy-dollar-a-month cold-water flat on Bank Street. Along the way, she had a few little triumphs, like a good role maybe once a year with some rag-tag theater that paid wages a mouse couldn't live on. And every now and then she'd get a little part in one of those TV commercials, which kept her going for a long time because they paid her again every thirteen weeks as long as the commercial was on the air, but now for the past six months, she told me, the pickings had been thin.

"People aren't going to the theater anymore," Alice said. "And I don't blame them. A Broadway musical costs fifteen dollars a seat and you'll probably get mugged afterward on Eighth Avenue trying to hail a cab. If you go *off* Broadway, down on East Fourth Street, you have to wade through winos and addicts just to get to the box office. They'll grab your purse or slash your pockets open with a razor blade. My cousin came to town last year, when I was doing *Hedda,* and he did his business down in Wall Street during the day and stayed in his hotel at night. He was afraid to go out on the streets."

"Why didn't he ask The Law for help?" I asked. She glared at me.

"We've been going through another business recession," she went on. "So TV commercials are getting scarcer, too. And, face it, I don't exactly look like Mrs. Average American Housewife anyway. Up to this year, I used to get the kooky character parts, but my wardrobe's getting a little ragged and wouldn't you know, I can't buy clothes off the rack. I have to go to those Tall Gal shops and pay another twenty dollars for the privilege of wearing styles that make me look like the Jolly Green Giant."

The burglaries hadn't helped, either. Her TV set went, along with the radio, the toaster, and even a secondhand sewing machine she'd hoped would help bring down her clothing budget. The extra locks on the door had cost her almost fifty dollars, and now her unemployment benefits were nearly gone.

"There's always welfare," she said. I knew she was lying. She'd never take charity, and that's what it is, in spite of what the politicians call it when they try and buy votes from those lazy fellers who sit back and live off other people's work.

Alice was scratching hard bottom, and that's no fooling. She thought she was still fighting, but I could tell that inside she'd given up. It was written in the soot she'd had on her face, in the grundgy clothes she wore, and in the three locks she'd used to set up a barricade between her and the rest of the world.

She was on the long slide, and I knew if I let loose she'd go all the way to the big crash at the bottom. The snow would be flying soon, and if I wasn't back in the Wyoming mountains before it hit, that'd be all she wrote until the spring thaw. But what choice did I have? Alice was one of mine now, and I couldn't run out on her while she was hurting.

"Listen, Alice," I said, "I ain't one for settling down, not anymore. Never was there a heartier sigh of relief breathed then when my three daughters took off and I was on my own again. So don't get to counting on me being around as a steady thing. I might leave in the morning, I might stay a week or even a month—but sooner or later, sure as sunrise, I'll be going."

"So go," she said. "What's keeping you?"

I didn't pay her no mind. She was just talking. "Seems to me," I said, "that most of the problems around here would get solved if there was just a little more money coming in."

"What are you thinking of? Holding up a bank?"

"No profit there. These days, all they got in the vault

is checks." I studied her. "You know, Alice, you said for a while there you made out pretty good with them TV commercials. How well are you connected with the people who make them?"

She spread her hands. "Pretty well. They still like me. It's just that nothing's come along."

"It ain't come along for you. How about for me? Do you figure that maybe I could peddle something on TV?"

She laughed. "*You*? Fred, you're not an actor."

"How about all them baseball players I see? Since when do you have to be an actor to talk about hair cream or razor blades?"

"It's crazy, Fred——"

"What do we have to lose? Listen, big woman, you take me on over and introduce me to the gent who hires folks for them TV commercials."

"But it doesn't work that way. You need composite pictures, a list of your credits, your union card. You have to audition——"

"What's audition?"

"The producer has to look you over and maybe ask you to read from the script."

"I reckon I can do that. Let's get moving."

Alice argued, but her heart wasn't in it, and that afternoon we caught a subway uptown and waded through the crowds to one of those skyscraper buildings where we took an elevator, which is something I haven't done very often. My ears popped on the way up, and my stomach felt uneasy, but I swallowed a couple of times and managed to keep a smile working. The ride didn't bother Alice at all, but then she was used to it.

Upstairs, we got out of the elevator into a room with floor-to-ceiling windows that made the place look like a diving board two hundred feet over the city. I wanted to grab onto something tight and yell for help.

I swallowed hard. "So this here is one of them advertising agencies."

"Fred," Alice whispered, "we shouldn't be here."

"How are we going to find out if they got any work unless we ask them?"

"But there's a procedure to follow. First you get an agent, and she sends you over for an audition, and——"

"Seems simpler just to ask." I went over to a handsome middle-aged woman behind a big desk and said, "Howdy, ma'am. I was wondering if maybe you had some of them TV commercial jobs open?"

She looked surprised, but she was polite enough. She had me sit down, and she filled in some kind of long green form. Mostly, she wrote down "nos," because every time she asked me if I had any experience or if I'd ever used a certain brand of toothpaste or shaving cream, that's what I had to say. Finally, she thanked me for coming in and promised me that she'd call if anything came up, which I knew right off was a lie, because I'd told her twice that there wasn't any phone where I could be reached. It was obvious to me from the first that she wasn't much more than a secretary and didn't have diddly-squat to say about anything important. But I kept smiling at her, because there wasn't any point to deviling her. She was only doing what they told her to.

Pretty soon Alice and me found ourselves back in the hall waiting for the elevator next to the ash trays filled with sand and the coffee table covered with magazines.

"I told you," Alice said. She looked real pretty, dressed up in a red shirt and a checkered skirt.

"We just made a bad start," I said. "We'll do better once I get my compass bearings."

"Oh, Fred, for Christ's sake!" Alice yelled. "I don't know why I let you talk me into this. We aren't up on top of old Devil Mountain stalking an antelope. This is *New York,* and you can't come on corny here because they simply won't buy it!"

I started to answer, but just then the elevator door opened and three old men got out. I mean, they was *old.* Maybe I had them on years, but when it comes to wear and tear, they outpointed me ten to one.

"Well, looky there," I said. "And I thought *I* was beat-up."

A young woman carrying a clipboard came out after them, glanced to the left, and said, "Room 2190. Follow me please, gentlemen."

"What's this 2190?" I hissed at Alice.

"It's the audition studio. But——"

"No buts. Let's go."

"Fred!"

"Hush up."

I fell in line behind the three old geezers. Alice brought up the rear. The fossils, all in a line like scurrying quail, followed the girl with the clipboard into a cork-lined room. I caught the door as it started to shut, held it for Alice, and we went inside, too.

There were six or seven people grouped around a table. Along one wall there was a row of folding metal chairs. I slid onto one, Alice took the one beside me, and we both sat still. The girl with the clipboard gave me a curious glance, but I avoided her eye.

A well-dressed man, maybe in his early forties, leaned over the end of the table and said, "Thanks for coming down, guys." The way he pronounced the word "guys" would have busted my jaw. "I hate to have you audition in front of a committee, but like they say, that's show biz. The client's here, and the director from the production house, and, of course, the copywriter. So do your best and be at your phone at six this evening. We'll call you all then, whether or not you get the job. And we shoot tomorrow."

One of the old men cleared his throat. "Why such short notice?"

Everyone glared at him. He wasn't grateful enough. "Because," said the man at the end of the table, patiently, "Charlie Bellows, who originally had the part, died yesterday of a heart attack, may he rest in peace."

"Oh," said the old man. He gave a broad smile. One less competitor to worry about.

"Who's first?" asked the man at the table.

"Laurence Morrison," said the girl with the clipboard.

Codger Number One stood up and, in a rich, deep voice, said, "Late of the Lincoln Center Repertory Company."

Alice and Me

"Right," said the man at the table. "I saw your *King Lear*. Wonderful stuff, Larry. Well, here's the pitch. You're suffering from piles, dig? Pain, itching, the *whole* thing." He gave a little laugh. "Sorry, ladies. Then you try our product, Deep Balm, and everything's swell. Your line is, 'Ah, blessed relief. No more tortured itching.' Got it?"

Laurence Morrison squinched up his face. He pressed his fingers against the top of his brow and mumbled to himself for a while, then said in a tightly clenched voice, "I think I'm ready."

A fat woman at the table, who wore an ugly flowered hat, leaned over and, in a voice that was deeper than Morrison's, said, "Have him hold the product."

A young man hustled over and gave Morrison a package of Deep Balm. The actor studied it like it was a solid gold nugget.

"Go ahead, Larry," said the man at the table. "Give it everything you've got."

Morrison held the package up alongside his cheek and, in a voice that sounded as if he were running for President, said, "Ah, blessed relief. No more tortured itching."

"Wonderful," said the man at the table. He looked around. "Boys and girls?"

The fat woman said, "Perhaps if he emphasized 'blessed' a little more."

The man nodded. "Larry? One more time."

"Ah, *blessed* relief. No more tortured itching."

"Terrific," said the man at the table.

The fat woman said, "Not so heavy on 'itching.' Punch up 'tortured.'"

51

The man at the table nodded. "Let's make this a take, Larry."

"Ah, *blessed* relief. No more *tortured* itching."

"Perfect," said the man at the table. "Okay, thanks, Larry. Glad you could come in. What are you doing next?"

"The title role in *Julius Caesar* for the Tyrone Guthrie Theater," said Morrison.

"Swell, wonderful," said the man. "I'll try to catch the opening."

"It's in Minneapolis," said the actor.

"Oh," said the man. "Well, we'll let you know, Larry."

The old actor bowed. Walking with stiff dignity, he left the room.

It took only a few minutes more for the other two codgers to recite, "Ah, *blessed* relief. No more *tortured* itching," and then everyone, including the girl with the clipboard, looked at me.

"I don't believe I know this gentleman," said the man at the table.

"He's not with *me,*" said the girl with the clipboard. "I thought *your* office brought him in."

I stood up and said, "Nobody brought me in. I just got in line and followed the parade."

"Well, see here," said the man at the table, "this isn't an open casting call. You have to be sent by an agent."

I picked up the bright green package of Deep Balm and studied it. "Does this stuff really work?"

The bullfrog-voiced woman said, "Of *course* it works."

"Well, why don't you say so? What's all this 'blessed relief' crap?"

"I beg your pardon?" said the man.

I tossed the package up into the air and caught it with a sharp slap of my hand. "Hot diggety damn! Now I can ride my hoss again!"

The man said, "Now, really."

The woman stared at me. "What did you say?"

"Just what I *would* say if I had me a bad case of the piles and your stuff dried them up. Hot diggety damn! Now I can ride my hoss again!"

The man looked around the room. "He's crazy. Call the cops."

"Just a minute," said the fat woman. "This is intriguing. Mr.——?"

"Jasper Whitecloud, ma'am. Two-fifths Cheyenne Indian on my Pa's side."

"Well, Mr. Whitecloud," she said, "I represent the manufacturers of Deep Balm, and I like the way you think. You went right to the seat of our problems." She glared around at the other folks in the room, and they all got fidgety and red in the face. "Something which this hundred-million-dollar advertising agency and its high-salaried executives seem unable to do. Mr. Whitecloud, you're hired."

"Well, ma'am, that's sounds fine. That is, if the terms are right."

"Union scale," said the man at the table.

The fat woman cleared her throat. "The terms will be right, Mr. Whitecloud. I can assure you of that."

The girl with the clipboard said, "We'll have to get

back to you, Mr. Whitecloud. If I could have your telephone number——"

"Don't have one," I said. "Wouldn't sit around it waiting for you to call even if I did." I started for the door. "Nice meeting you folks. Too bad you can't seem to make up your minds."

"Don't go, Mr. Whitecloud," said the fat lady. "I've made up *my* mind. You're hired. And the agency will go along with my decision, I'm sure."

"My sentiments exactly, Sarah," said the man at the table.

"We're shooting at MPO Studio on West Forty-fourth Street," said the clipboard girl. "If you'll stop at my office on the way out——"

"Who are you, little lady?" I asked.

Flushing, she said, "Why, I'm the agency's casting director for this product. I——"

"Thank you kindly, but no thanks," I said, giving her a broad wink. "I heard all about them casting couches you folks got."

Quickly, Alice said, "I know where MPO is. Is an eight A.M. call all right?"

"Perfect, miss," said the fat woman named Sarah. "Is Mr. Whitecloud your grandfather, dear?"

"Alice here's my child bride," I said, trying not to grin and mess it all up. "I wore out nine wives, so I figured I'd better get me a young one this time."

"Very sensible," said the fat woman.

"We'll see you in the morning at MPO," Alice said, dragging me toward the door.

When we were in the self-service elevator, she collapsed against the wall, laughing. "Fred! How did you do it?"

"Easy," I said. "You could see there wasn't anyone in that room able to make a bigger decision than picking out a necktie. They was swimming around in all directions. I just gave them a strong opinion to latch onto."

"You're wonderful," she said. "Do you know what an account like that is *worth?*"

"I figure I ought to do good. What did you say the union scale was? A hundred and fifty a day? That's pretty good pay for just one day's work."

"But that's only the beginning," she said. "They'll pay you that for each spot you shoot, even if you make four or five the same day. And if they all start running nationally, you can take in a thousand, maybe fifteen hundred dollars a week. For months. Maybe years."

"Well, that's right nice," I said. "But let's not count those chickens before they come home to roost."

She fixed me with a stare. "What's with this Jasper Whitecloud routine?"

I chucked her under the chin. "Lady, would you use *your* right name on a salve for itchy assholes?"

FIVE

Now, I know you aren't really interested in how I got rich in the TV commercial business, and the only reason I bring it up is to explain how, all of a sudden, Alice and me was rolling in money. But if you want to take a moral out of it, I guess it goes to show that if a man wants to hustle, there ain't no cause for him to go around busting into apartments or mugging people in the park.

It took me two whole days to get Alice out of that flea-trap on Bank Street, because I didn't get my check until the end of the day I made them Deep Balm commercials, and then it took another whole day to locate a nice place to live.

Getting my money was the hardest of the two. The way people hang onto it, you'd think that green stuff was covered with glue.

Alice and me went over to that MPO place at eight in the morning like they said. I'd expected a movie studio, with gates and a uniformed guard outside, and handymen shoving artificial trees around. But this was just another skyscraper building with regular elevators that took us to the sixth floor where we wandered around narrow halls until we came to a big room filled with lights and guys drinking coffee from paper cups.

The fat lady was already there, and she came over.

"We never did get properly introduced, Mr. Whitecloud," she boomed. "I'm Sarah Wilson, and I represent the St. Croix Pharmaceutical Company."

"Miz Sarah," I said. "One look yesterday and I could see that you was the boss, plain as the nose on my face. And I'm just as proud to meet you. Now why don't we get on with it? I come here to work, so just point out what you want me to do."

She laughed. "Don't be in such a hurry, Mr. Whitecloud."

"Call me Jasper, boss lady."

"All right, Jasper. First, you've got to go to your dressing room and a girl will put your makeup on——"

"Makeup? No, ma'am, I don't think we're putting on no makeup."

Sarah looked over at Alice. "Mrs. Whitecloud, hasn't your husband ever been on a set before?"

Alice touched my shoulder. "Fred—Jasper—everybody uses makeup. Jimmy Stewart, Raymond Burr, even John Wayne wears makeup."

"I don't want to look like Jimmy Stewart or John Wayne, and I sure in hell don't want to look like Raymond Burr," I said, glaring at Sarah Wilson. "Boss lady, is it your idea that I should?"

"Not at all, Jasper. The company likes you just the way you are. But——"

"Then whose idea is it that I get myself all painted up like a whore in church?"

Sarah thought for a moment. "You know," she said, "I'm not even sure myself. Excuse me."

She left. Alice tugged at my sleeve. "Watch it," she said. "You're going to blow it. You can ruin everything. Do you know why you've got to wear makeup? Because the union says the studio's got to have makeup people on the set, and the producer's not going to pay a makeup man for just sitting around doing nothing."

"Makeup *man*? I thought it was a girl."

"Sometimes it's a girl, sometimes a man. Fred, what does it matter?"

"It matters to *me*. A girl is bad enough, but do you think I'd let some *man* smear lipstick on me?"

"Oh, Fred, settle down. You'd let a male barber shave you, wouldn't you?"

"Big woman, don't you figure that maybe there's a difference between a straight razor and a tube of lipstick? Or is it that you ain't never used lipstick yourself, and just don't know?"

This was a cheap shot, because Alice had fixed herself up real pretty this morning. But she *had* gone a little shy on the lipstick and I always liked my women ripe and red.

Alice glared at me, but just then Sarah Wilson came back with a nervous, skinny guy whose bald head reflected the studio lights.

"Jasper, this is our director, Mike Rosen. Mike, like

I told you, Jasper here has a skin problem. He's been out of doors so long that he gets an allergenic reaction to makeup. Does he really need it?"

Mike Rosen squinted at me. "He's got pretty good skin tone. Maybe a little on the red side, though."

"Can't you correct that in the video transfer?"

"Maybe. But that'll throw everything else off a little. If the shader moves him toward the blue side, your package color may shift over toward the magenta."

"Let's do it," said Sarah. "Hire a hand model for the product close-ups and use regular makeup so they'll look all right. But go with Jasper the way he is."

Mike Rosen nodded and went over to talk with a fat little man who was scurrying around with a clipboard. Everybody in the TV business seemed to carry a clipboard. Sarah turned toward me. "Your first lesson in craft union relations," she said. "If I'd told Mike that we *had* to shoot without makeup, he'd have made a federal case out of it and screwed around with lighting changes and filters, and we'd have blown most of the morning. But instead, I let him know we had a problem. It became *his* problem, and now he's laying it all on the shoulders of the poor assistant director whose job it is to solve *all* problems."

"Yes, ma'am," I said. "I can see that you sure know how to get things done, and that's good, because Alice and me, we've got a problem too."

"Really?" The friendship had leaked completely out of Miz Sarah's voice.

"It's like this. According to the scripts they gave me

last night, we're going to make us four of them TV commercials today, isn't that right?"

"That's correct." Miz Sarah was now one real suspicious lady.

"Well, Alice here has shown me how I'll get paid a hundred and fifty dollars apiece, more or less, for each and every one of those commercials."

"That's right. Less, naturally, federal withholding tax, state and city income tax, social security, pension and welfare, medical, unemployment benefits, and, of course, your dues and initiation for SAG."

"SAG? What's SAG?"

"S-A-G. Screen Actor's Guild." Sarah Wilson batted her eyes at me. "That's the usual arrangement, Mr. Whitecloud. What's bothering you?"

"Well, I did me a little figuring in my head, and it come to me that by the time you folks get done with all that withholding business, I'm going to be withheld right down to the bottom of the barrel."

She smiled tightly. "Well, of course, *we* had no way of knowing that you didn't belong to the union, and yes, the initiation fee *is* a rather large deduction. But you must remember, you'll be receiving a handsome residual check every thirteen weeks."

"Yes ma'am, that's what Alice told me. It seems like you aim to use these here TV commercials an awful lot, ain't that right?"

"Saturation, Mr. Whitecloud. We intend to saturate the nation."

"Like I said, ma'am you can call me Jasper."

Quick as a flash, she shot back, "Not until I find out what it is you want, Mr. Whitecloud."

"Well," I told her, "I figure that as complicated as our problem seems to me, why a smart lady like you ought to be able to work it out real fast. I mean, this St. Croix Pharmaceutical Company of yours is solvent, ain't it?"

"Solvent!" she flared. "Our stock is listed on the Big Board."

"Don't know just what *that* is," I said. "But, by golly, it sure *sounds* solvent, don't it? The Big Board. That's impressive. Well, I'm glad, because if things is going so good for you, then I reckon you can fix us up with a little advance."

"Certainly," she said. "If you need a hundred dollars or so——"

"I was thinking more in the neighborhood of five thousand."

"Dollars?"

I nodded.

She sat down. "That's some neighborhood, Mr. Whitecloud."

"From what you've told me, ma'am, I'll be entitled to that and maybe more even before them first thirteen weeks is up."

"What's that got to do with it?"

"Well, it isn't like I was asking for a loan. It's my own money, ain't it?"

"Well, perhaps you might say that it *will* be yours, one day down the road."

I smiled at her. "Since we're traveling the same road, Miz Sarah, why can't we forget about the details and just transfer some of that money right here at the starting gate."

Firmly, she said, "I'm sorry. We simply do not pay in *advance*."

"Miz Sarah, you don't seem to have no trouble asking me to work in advance."

"That's different," she said. "I'm sorry, Mr. White-cloud."

"Why not? I thought your company had plenty of money in the bank. You're listed on that Big Board, ain't you? Seems to me you could afford to be a little generous. After all, Alice and me, we ain't got no money at all."

"Perhaps we could arrange something in the area of a few hundred dollars," she said. "But five *thousand*? What on earth do you want with all that money?"

"Well, maybe you wouldn't understand," I said. "Unless you been broke, you won't know what I mean. But having just a little cash in your pocket, that's worse than having none at all. If a body's stony broke, why there ain't no lower he can go, so it don't bother him too much. But what can I do with a piddling little dab of money? You can't have no fun, counting every little penny, trying to stretch it out to make a nickel. Maybe I might want to buy a used car, but with what you want to give me, that'd blow a hole in my bankroll so big you could drive the *car* through it. And maybe I want to buy Alice here a few pretties." Alice glared at me, and I gave her a wink. "But I can't see no way we'd be comfortable at all without five thousand dollars or so."

Sarah Wilson had clenched her lips, and her knuckles were white from making fists. "I'm sorry," she said, "I simply do not have the authority to pay such a sum in advance."

I looked around the crowded studio. "Miz Sarah, what do you figure this studio setup costs you by the hour? You've got a big operation here, look at all these people, and the equipment, and that makeup man you got hid back in my dressing room. What does it run? Two thousand dollars an hour? Maybe three? That'd come to twenty thousand dollars for the day." I whistled. "My, my, you advertising people surely do throw money around. Alice told me that sometimes you'll spend fifty or sixty thousand dollars on one little minute TV commercial. And since you already got all these people standing around, I reckon you've got to pay them whether or not I work, don't you?" I smiled down on her. "Do you reckon your boss is in his office yet, Miz Sarah?"

"Why?"

"Well, since you ain't got the say-so, maybe you ought to call *him,* and get his okay to pay me that five thousand."

"I couldn't possibly disturb Mr. St. Croix with such a stupid request."

"I'm sorry to hear you say that, ma'am, because until that money is in my hot little hand, I ain't going in front of them cameras. Nowhere, nohow."

She almost choked. "We'll sue. We've got a contract."

"Go ahead and sue. What can you take off me? I ain't got nothing except what I'm wearing. Besides, I never signed no contract yet, or them tax forms you give me neither. I'm particular what I put my name to. Now, what do you say, Miz Sarah?"

"This is blackmail, you scheming old crook."

"That'll just cost you an extra thousand dollars, Miz Sarah. My price is six thousand dollars now."

She started to answer, tightened her lips, and headed for the telephone. "I'll be right back," she half screamed.

The minute Miz Sarah was gone, Alice hissed, "You're crazy! They'll fire you."

"Every word I said was the gospel truth, Alice. I ain't asking for a loan, just that they give me what's rightfully mine."

"They won't give it to you. They can't. If they did, every actor in town would——"

She stopped. I grinned at her. "Would what, big woman? Most folks couldn't get away with what I just pulled. They'd be scared, holding back. You can't run a bluff on something like this. But I wasn't bluffing. I meant it, every word. And that fat woman knew it. She won't blow all this overhead. No chance, Alice. And what if she did? What have I lost? I didn't have anything to start with, so I ain't got nothing to lose."

Alice sighed. "What am I going to do with you?"

Sarah Wilson came back. She said, "I spoke with Mr. St. Croix. He agrees with me that you are a thieving, lying, conniving old crook who'd steal the nickels off his dead mother's eyelids."

"Now, *that*'ll cost you——"

"I know." She glowered at me. "I asked for an extra thousand dollars just so I could say it."

SIX

The bank gave me a real hard time cashing my seven-thousand-dollar check. I was just as glad Alice wasn't with me, because I had to get a little rough. I started out with the fat uniformed guard, asked him where I could cash a check, and he pointed me to a long line in front of the only window that was open. I stood in it for around half an hour, and worked my way up to the window. I handed the check to the woman teller. She glanced at it and shoved it back at me.

"I'm sorry," she said. "I can't cash this without an officer's approval."

"That's all right," I said. "I can wait. Go get his approval."

"You'll have to do that yourself," she told me. "You should have done it before you got in line."

"Is this what always happens? You got to get an officer's okay before cashing one of these things?"

"Yes, sir. You can see Mr. Grimsby, over there behind the railing."

I stepped back out of line and went over to the guard. He gave me a shit-eating grin.

"Did you know that I'd need an officer's approval before I could cash my check?"

He shifted his weight. "You didn't ask me that. All you asked was *where* to cash one."

"That's mighty funny, bub. Is that what you do to forget you're nothing but a fat old man with bad breath who they put out here to dress up the joint for the paying customers?"

His hand brushed the butt of his revolver. "Better not cause any trouble, mister."

I stepped up close. "Go ahead, fatso," I whispered. "I dearly hope you'll try to pull that gun so I can shove it down your throat. Now before I *really* get mad, didn't I hear you say you were sorry for wasting my time?"

He glared at me, but his face was starting to sweat.

I moved in a little closer. "I just can't hear you," I said, very low.

Grudgingly, almost without moving his lips, he mumbled, "Sorry. I made a mistake."

"Don't we all?" I said, stepping back. "Just be careful, hey?"

I kept a watch on him from the corner of my eye as I went over to the junior vice-president's desk, but the guard didn't make a move. I smiled. He'd have to go to the bathroom, real soon.

I put the check down in front of Mr. Grimsby, the junior vice-president. He was a dark, middle-aged man with a thin, black, pencil moustache.

"I stood in line ten minutes and then the girl said I needed your okay to cash this here check."

He gave me a long, examining look, for which I couldn't blame him, because I was still wearing the work clothes I'd left Kansas in, and while they was clean, they was pretty rough for the inside of a bank on New York City's Park Avenue.

"Certainly, sir," he said, taking the check. He looked at it, and his eyes got wide. "Seven *thousand* dollars?"

"That's what it says."

He held it up to the light. "Yes, it certainly does." He looked up at me. "Just who *are* you, sir?"

"It's writ right there on the check. Cash."

"But that's not your name."

"If the check's made out to cash, my name's Cash."

"But——"

"It's good, ain't it? I mean, the check."

"The instrument is drawn on an account in this bank, yes, and of course there's no question of its being covered by funds. But you must understand, sir, that we just can't hand out seven thousand dollars to any Tom, Dick, or Harry who walks in off the street."

"I get you. It *ain't* good."

"I didn't say that, sir. If you will just present it through normal banking channels by depositing it to your own account, the check will be paid in due course."

"I ain't got no account. But this check tells you to pay the bearer, whoever he happens to be, seven thousand dollars. I don't see no fine print that says it got to come to you by mail or through another bank. Now, if it ain't any good, just tell me and I'll fix the guy who give it to me, this Mr. St. Croix, and naturally that ain't any of your problem. But if it *is* good and you're giving me the merry runaround, well then, mister, you've got real trouble."

His lips tightened and his hand touched the telephone. But he didn't pick it up. "Are you making a threat, sir?"

I shook my head. "No indeed. All I'm saying is that I want my money. So why don't you give it to me, and I'll be on my way."

"I'll have to see your identification, Mr.——?"

"The name is Cash."

"Please, sir," he said, "can't I make you understand that a stranger, particularly one—ah—attired so casually as yourself, simply cannot stroll into a bank and demand seven thousand dollars in cash? Now, for instance, if you had an account here——"

"I get it," I said. "Your price for giving me my own money is for me to let it lay here for you fellers to use."

"That's the usual way of doing business."

"Well, it ain't *my* usual way. Can I use your telephone?" He hesitated, and I said, "It's a local call, and I'll pay you the dime."

Reluctantly, he handed me the receiver and pressed a button. It lit up, and I heard an operator say, "Your call, please?"

"Lady, I don't know the number, but I want you to get me the St. Croix Pharmaceutical Company, and then I want to talk to Mr. St. Croix himself."

Mr. Grimsby grabbed the phone from me and hissed into it, "Cancel that call!" He hung up. "What do you think you're doing?"

"If you'll look close," I said, "you'll see that Mr. St.

Croix himself signed that check. I figured he might be interested in hearing how slow you folks are in paying off on it."

Mr. Grimsby was sweating. "I wasn't aware that you knew Mr. St. Croix."

"Well, live and learn," I said. "If you won't let me use your phone, it don't matter. I've still got my dime, so I reckon I'll go find me a pay telephone."

"That won't be necessary," Mr. Grimsby said, scribbling something on the back of the check. "You should have *said* you were personally acquainted with Mr. St. Croix. Anything we can do to be of service. . . ."

He handed me the check. "If you'll just present this to the teller."

I shook my head. Alarmed, he asked, "What's wrong now?"

"Mr. Grimsby," I told him, "I already stood in that goddamned line once today. I figure this time it's *your* turn."

Now that I had my cash money, I started out to look for a place to live. Naturally, the first thing I did was to read the want ads, but the prices there curled my hair.

> *3 1/2 minipad, 71st off Lex,*
> *elvtr, drmn, utilities. $925.*

Nine hundred bucks a month just for a place to sleep! I didn't waste my time reading any more of that stuff. The prices in *The New York Times* weren't for ordinary people like Alice and me. I wondered who read it, anyway, with its funny little headlines and tiny printing and all them ads for ladies' clothes. Probably a bunch of female midgets with magnifying glasses and nine hundred dollars to spend on a place to sleep.

Alice had mentioned that the West Side, up in the eighties, was an area she wouldn't mind living in, so I waved down a cab and got in.

"Take me up to West Eightieth Street, over near the river," I said, but the driver didn't hear me because there was a sheet of bulletproof glass between him and me. It pushed me back like a prisoner in the back seat of a squad car.

"What did you say?" he yelled.

I told him where I wanted to go again, and he still didn't hear me, so I got out and stood by his window.

"What's the matter?" I asked. "Are you afraid of me?"

"The mayor made us put that glass in," he said. "It's supposed to protect us from the niggers."

"The last time I looked my face was white," I said. "Besides, what have you got against niggers?"

He laughed in a sour way. "Wait until one pulls you over late at night and says to take him to some dark corner in Harlem, and all the way up he sits back there fingering a knife in his pocket. I quit hacking at night, just for that reason. We've got these lock boxes, but you can't make change if you put everything in them, and those spades know it, so they'll still knock you over, just for the ones and change in your pockets."

"Don't you ever get held up by white men?" I asked.

He hesitated. "Sometimes. But that's different."

"How so?"

"Well, they ain't so likely to kill you."

"Didn't I read the other day about how three white

men held up a bank down on Broadway, and took hostages, and when the cops pulled them over, they cut those hostages' throats?"

"Listen," he said loudly, "the meter's running. Where do you want to go?"

"Never mind," I said. "I figure I'll find me a driver who ain't scared of me."

"You owe me sixty cents!" he yelled.

"No I don't. It's too bad you started charging before you started moving. Maybe next time you'll slow down a little and think."

I walked off. He shook his fist at me and shouted, "You know what you are? You're a lousy kike!"

First I was a nigger, and now I was a kike. Maybe I could make wop before the day was over.

I waved down another cab that didn't have one of those barricades in the middle and we scooted uptown pretty fast. This driver was smart; he didn't shoot off his mouth complaining how small his last tip had been, and he didn't fumble with the change hoping I'd forget it. I threw him an extra dollar, and he said, "Thanks."

"Don't mention it. Hey, mister, do I look Italian to you?"

"What?"

"Never mind."

Most of the buildings in this neighborhood were solid, brown chunks of stone and metal, all looking pretty much alike. I poked my head into a couple of lobbies, and the first two smelled of cabbage cooking, so I passed them by. I worked my way up to West End Avenue before I hit pay dirt.

A swarthy man grabbed my shoulder as I leaned inside the entrance and growled, "Where the hell do you think *you're* going?"

"I'm looking for the super," I told him.

"I'm the super, and we don't need any more bums around here. Move it."

"I thought I might like an apartment in a building like this one," I said.

"No way," he said.

I took out a handful of fifty-dollar bills and riffled them like a deck of cards. His eyes bugged out.

"It's an awful nice building," I said.

"We're full up," he mumbled, eyes glued to the money.

"Are you sure we can't work something out?"

"Sorry," he said. He meant it. He was so hungry for those bills that he was bleeding inside. "Lots of people offer me a few bucks to put them on top of the list, but I can't do a thing."

I peeled off eight fifties. "I bet you those lots of people you mentioned never handed you four hundred dollars in cash money."

I stuffed the bills down inside his breast pocket. "I'll be back in an hour," I said. "Why don't you help me if you can, and if you can't, then I'll just take my money back."

"I'm not sure I can do anything" he said. But the money had vanished. For good, I'd bet on that.

"Try. My name is Fred."

"Call me Bernie. Listen, Mac, maybe I *can* do something. But I'll need more than an hour."

"How much more?"

"It's eleven now. You come back at two. I've got to make some phone calls."

"Will you have something to show me at two?"

"I think so."

"Think yes or no. I've got to call somebody myself."

"Okay. Yes. I'm almost sure."

"Almost ain't good enough, Bernie. Make it yes or no."

"Yes. Okay, yes."

"Fine. Two o'clock, Bernie."

I walked up to a bar on Broadway and called Alice.

"Let's have dinner, big woman," I said.

"Dinner? It's not even noon. Oh, you mean lunch, don't you?"

"We call it dinner, but if you want to say lunch, that's okay with me. Come on, lady, we got to start celebrating."

"You got the money!"

"Could be."

"Fred! You really got it!"

"Where do you want to eat?"

"Well, where are you now?"

"Broadway and Eighty-fourth Street."

She hesitated. "Do you like Japanese food?"

"Never tried it. But I like rice."

"Over on Columbus and Sixty-ninth, there's a little place called the Sakura. It's cheap ——"

"Never mind about cheap."

"And good, and I think you'll love it. I'll meet you there in half an hour. I'll bring along the wine, because they don't have a booze license."

"Good," I said. "Now, you take a cab, Alice. But not one of them with that bulletproof glass, understand?"

"Fred, what on earth are you talking about."

"Never mind. You just hurry on, you hear me, woman?"

"I will."

I hung up and killed some time walking over to the restaurant, looking in store windows, especially the big hardware store at the corner of Seventy-ninth and Amsterdam. If I could only have moved that store to Alaska in 1944, I would have become a millionaire. All those gadgets and pieces of electric gear and equipment were enough to drive a good mechanical engineer up the wall.

Of course, we weren't only engineers up there. For nearly a year, I buddied up with a couple of guys who were part of a sniper outfit training near Fairbanks. Talk about rough, those good old boys used to shoot cigarettes out of each other's mouths just for target practice. I guess I learned as much about shooting from them as I did in the first fifty years of my life.

One of the boys we called Mose, because every time he got drunk he come into the barracks and started kicking over the butt cans full of sand and cigarettes. Mose was the coolest man with a rifle I have ever seen. Him and me, we went out rabbit hunting one Saturday, and I was using my .22 Savage. I got three in a row, two of them on the run, and I felt pretty good about that, until Mose shook his head and said, "You ain't breathing right. And you're burning in the sight picture."

That got my back up. I'd hit all three, hadn't I?

"What the hell do you mean?" I asked. "I'm breathing like I always breathe, and I don't know what burning in the sight pictures signifies. I just put that old showshoe right there on top of my front sight and squoze off."

"You're not a bad shot," he admitted. "In fact, you're pretty good. But you're better on the running shots than you are when the target's sitting still."

I didn't say anything. He was right. The two rabbits running had been hit right through the head. I took the sitting one a little low. Just like I'd shot old Mr. Eskimo.

"Why do you think that is?" I asked.

He shrugged. "My guess is that on the running shots, you're instinct shooting. Just pulling up and aiming that piece like it's part of your arm." He nodded toward a distant bush. "Use your hand. Point at that bush and hold it. *Now!*"

I snapped my hand up, finger pointing. Mose slid down under my elbox and looked.

"You're right on," he said. "That's why your snap shooting is so good. It's instinct to point your finger accurately, and that's the same way you point your weapon."

"What's wrong with that?"

"Nothing. But where you fall apart is when you take time to *aim* your shots. Oh, they're not bad, Fred. You're still hitting. But it's sloppy shooting. It'd get you killed by a countersniper if you were in my line of work."

"What am I doing wrong?"

"Well, let's look at what you're doing right, first. Sight your piece."

I pulled up the .22 and looked down its barrel.

Mose nodded. "You know how to use your eye. You got it in there close to that rear sight, three inches or so. That's the right eye relief. And you're looking straight on—you aren't trying to sight out of the corner of your eye or over the bridge of your nose. That'd give you eye strain and involuntary eye movements that cut down on your accuracy. You're fine there, Fred. But you're burning in the sight picture."

"That's twice you said that, and I still don't get it."

"You're fixing your vision on the sight picture too long. What that does is to ruin your eye's area of perception. You ever stare at a light bulb and then look at a blank wall?"

"Sure," I said. "You can still see the bulb, even though it ain't there."

"Right. The same thing happens when you stare at a target too long. There ain't no need to hold that picture so long. When you get lined up, squeeze off."

"Maybe that's why I been holding so long, I didn't feel I was lined up as good as I could get."

He shook his head. "You never will be, unless you've got a sandbag rest. What you got to do is wait until the sights swing over your target and let her go. I try to make little circles, that keep crossing what I'm shooting at. You can't ever be a hundred percent on, but you can come awful close. You got a clip in that thing?"

I slipped it in. "I do now."

"See the white blaze on that pine tree? Sit down and put a group of three into it."

I did. Like he said, I couldn't hold steady on the blaze all the time, so I tried to squeeze off every time the sights come around. When I was done, I started to get up.

He pressed down on my shoulder. "Stay there."

"I wanted to see how I did."

"You hit the blaze. But the group isn't very tight. Now let's work on your breathing. I guess you're sharp enough to know that if you breathe when you're trying to aim, the rise and fall of your chest will move the rifle vertically."

"Hell, yes," I said. "I hold my breath."

"But the wrong way," he said. "What you're doing is sucking in a breath and holding it, and that puts pressure on your diaphragm. You tense up, and that hurts your accuracy."

"Well, what am I *supposed* to do?"

"Your respiratory cycle lasts four to five seconds. But it only takes you a couple of seconds to inhale, and a couple more to exhale. So there's a pause between each cycle of two or three seconds. And you can stretch that pause out to last ten or fifteen seconds without getting uncomfortable. What you do to hold your breath properly for shooting is to inhale normally, and exhale the same, and then stop, right then, with your lungs empty. If you ain't finished lining up, do it, and squeeze off. All your breathing muscles are relaxed, and you'd be surprised how much more accurate you'll be. Try three more."

I did, holding my breath the way he'd said, and then we went up to look at the tree.

Mose pointed at three holes scattered around the rim

of the blaze. "These are your first three. Good enough to kill a rabbit, but not good enough to be a sniper." He covered three more with the palm of his hand. "These are the last three. Not bad for iron sights. I think you've got promise."

I cussed him a little, but I was pleased inside, and from that day on, my shooting improved with every round I fired.

Too bad Mose didn't take his own advice. I heard, later, that he tried to shoot a Jap tank commander's head off at six hundred yards, missed, and they turned the tank's 105 cannon on Mose and blasted him into little pieces.

A man in shirt sleeves came out of the hardware store. "Looking for anything special?" he asked.

"No thanks," I said. "Not unless you got an old Jap tank lying around."

He gave me a funny look, and I moved on. I wandered down Columbus Avenue, past the shuttered store fronts and the overflowing garbage cans. I may have seen dirtier cities, but I can't remember where.

At Seventy-second Street, over on the far corner, I saw a big black man sidle up to an old black woman who was waiting for the light to change. Just as the green "Walk" sign went on, he grabbed her purse so hard that the strap around her wrist broke. He charged across the street, right toward me, and when he went past, I stuck out my foot and he fell over it and skidded along the dirty sidewalk on his face. He dropped the purse, and I scooped it up and backed away, putting one of them green newsstands at my back. The big black man got up quickly, glared at me, and spat, "You honky muthah!" and took off. I was so busy watching him that I didn't see the old woman come up alongside me until she started bashing me with her fists and screaming, "Gimme my purse, you white bastard!"

I handed it over and got the hell out of there. She kept yelling after me, and I was damned glad to get on down the street and out of sight before the cops came. If they *ever* came.

"Why are you doing all this for me?" Alice asked. We were drinking warm red wine and eating little rice balls in the Jap restaurant.

"Let's say because it gives me pleasure," I said. "I ain't had nobody to do for in an awful long time."

She touched my hand. "Don't talk like that. You'll get me all snively."

"Go ahead and snivel. It's good for you."

She sipped her wine. "And you've really got a new apartment?"

"*You've* got a new apartment."

She tried to protest, and I cut her off. "What time is it?"

"Almost two."

"We'd better get moving."

I paid the check and we walked up to Eighty-fourth Street.

Bernie was waiting. "Mac, are you ever in luck."

"I thought I might be."

"When you was here before, I remembered that Mrs. Houghton, up in 12-B, was still in the hospital. I checked out her records, and like I figured, she's three months behind in her rent and the only reason old Churchill, he's the landlord, ain't evicted her already was because she was sick and he's got a soft heart."

Alice clutched my arm. "Fred!" she said. "We can't take a sick woman's apartment."

"Don't worry, lady," said good old Bernie, my wad of fifty-dollar bills obviously burning a hole in his pocket. "The apartment's already empty." He pointed through the door at a moving truck outside. "They're taking out the last of the furniture right now."

"Did she decide to leave?" I asked.

"Not exactly. I called the hospital right after you left, and what do you know, the old lady kicked off last night. They didn't know who to notify, that's why we hadn't already got the news. The minute I heard, I called the storage people. The old girl didn't have any relatives that I know about, but if someone turns up, they can claim the stuff down at the warehouse. And meanwhile, the apartment is vacant, just like I said." Bernie gave me a wide wink.

Alice pushed up closer to me. I looked at Bernie, and I didn't like him very much. "Is that the way things are done around here?" I asked.

"Well, what do you expect, Mac? Should I just seal up the door and put a black wreath on it? Listen, I thought you were anxious to get a place. I tried to do you a favor. This building is rent-controlled. Do you know what I could sell that lease for? The old dame's been in there since the war, so even with a fifteen percent increase, the rent's still only one sixty."

"Fred," said Alice, "I don't want it. Not like this."
I squoze her shoulder. "We might as well look at it.
Like Bernie said, he wouldn't have any trouble giving
it to somebody else."

So we went up in the elevator, and the apartment
was spacious and airy, and luckily the movers had already gotten most of the personal stuff out. Alice fell in
love with the place right off, and I slipped her enough
money to pay a month's rent and a month's security.

"You don't want my name on the lease," I told her.
"Not with my traveling habits being what they are."

Alarmed, she said, "You're not going, are you? Not
yet, please, Fred!"

"Don't fret," I said. "I'll stick around a while longer.
But right now, I want to hustle downstairs and talk to
them moving fellers, so they can bring your stuff right
over here today."

SEVEN

Well, that just about brings us up to where the real trouble started. I've told you all about Alice and me so's you'd know how we was *before*. I can see that it don't seem to bother you none talking to me now, so I reckon you won't really believe I'm all them things the newspapers said I am. And I'd swear to you on a stack of Bibles that Alice was just as sweet a girl as she could be. That may make it a little hard for you to understand how we could do what we did, but stick with me and I think you'll get there.

Alice had been knocked around pretty good before I met up with her, and while it toughened her, it didn't make her mean like you'd expect. She was one complete hunk of woman, all the way, and even now with what's happened, all I can say is that I'm real proud to have known her. What happened to her wasn't her fault.

One thing about the big city, you don't get shoved around or beat up or mugged because of anything in particular that you did, but only because you just happened to *be* there. Stick 'em up, mister, no hard feelings. The city don't do nobody any favors, it's nine million accident cases, all looking for a place to happen.

Mine happened the first night we were living in the new apartment. We'd gotten ourselves settled in good, had a couple of beers, and were watching the new color TV set I'd bought up on Broadway as a housewarming present for Alice.

"Fred!" she scolded when she saw it, "you've got to *stop* this. You're spending all your money."

"Plenty more where that come from," I said. "So long as folks have got itchy assholes."

"You can't depend on that, Fred. Getting a series of spots like this series of Deep Balm commercials is like lightning striking. It may never come near you again."

I goosed her in the ribs. "Now, see here, big woman, don't you start talking like a wife. Nagging's one thing I won't abide."

That made her mad. I could see that in the tightness around her lips. But she had the good sense to keep quiet. I felt a little sorry for leaning on her. After all, she was just trying to look out for me.

"You know, lady," I said, trying to make peace, "there's just one thing wrong with this celebration we're having."

"What?"

I patted her fanny. "We ought to be drinking us some sippin' whiskey instead of this beer."

She busted out laughing. "You're terrible! What does

money do in your pockets, anyway? Undergo spontaneous combustion?"

I took out the wad and riffled through it. I still had around six thousand dollars left. "It looks cool enough to me," I said. "Cool and green as a creek under the spruce trees."

"Fred! You ought to put that money into a bank."

"Put it *in* a bank? Big woman, you'll never know the aggravation I had just trying to get it *out* of a bank. No, sirree."

"Well, at least hide it somewhere. You can't walk around with seven thousand dollars in your, pocket."

I started to tell her that it was more like six, but instead, I peeled off a few fifties for myself and handed her the rest. "Here," I said. "*You* hide it."

She tried to push the wad back at me. "I don't want your money, Fred."

"I'm not giving it to you. All I want is for you to put it away someplace for safekeeping."

"It's too much of a responsibility. I can't even take care of my *own* money." She made an impatient gesture. "All I said was that you ought to be more careful. I wasn't hinting that you hand it over to me."

I tickled her under the chin. "I know you wasn't, Alice. Just do me the favor, all right? And meanwhile, since we ain't got us a telephone yet, I'll trot down and get us a bottle of the good drinking stuff."

Alice tried to thank me, and tried to kiss me, and I wouldn't let her do neither, because I *did* all of a sudden have me a genuine craving for some good sour mash bourbon, and if I let her sidetrack me I knew where we'd end up. That could wait until later.

I told her I'd be right back, and let myself out.

The clerk at the liquor store looked suspiciously at the fifty I gave him.

"What's the matter?" I asked.

"Is this bill good?"

I held up a bottle of Jack Daniels. "Is *this* good?"

"Sure it's good."

"Who says so?"

"The distillery says so, the distributor says so. *I* say so. What's that got to do with this fifty-dollar bill?"

"The United States Treasury says it's good, the bank says it's good, and *I* say it's good, and I got five or six more of them here and if you'll look, you'll see that the serial numbers are all different. Is that enough for you, bub?"

"Don't holler at *me,* old-timer. I just work here, and the boss don't like big bills."

"Too damned bad. That's all I got."

"I'll take a check."

"You'll take money or nothing."

He snapped the crisp new paper of the fifty with his fingernail. "It's okay, I guess." He rang up the sale and started making change.

"Thank you all to hell and gone," I said, picking up my money and stuffing it in my pants pocket.

I put the bottle of Jack under my arm and headed back to the apartment building. The lobby seemed empty when I walked in, but I guess it wasn't, because just as I pushed the elevator button, something hard and meaty pressed itself against my windpipe and squoze my breath clean off.

I heard a deep voice say, "Doan you move, baby, or ah'll break yoah muthafuggin neck."

I squirmed around anyway, but I was helpless in that murderous grip. The whiskey bottle slipped out of my hand and, distantly, I heard it smash on the tiled floor. Everything went red and hazy, and I felt my knees buckling under me. There came the sound of my pants pocket ripping as a big hand tore the fabric. I tried to stomp on a foot, kick an ankle, *anything*. But the life was draining out of me, and I couldn't move. So this was dying. All I felt, though, was anger that I couldn't mark my murderer up a little before I went.

Then the elevator door opened and there was good old Bernie with a mop and a pail of water. He straightened up in surprise, yelled, "What the hell's going on here?" and let fly with the mop handle.

The pressure at my throat relaxed, and I threw myself forward, bowling poor Bernie over like a startled tenpin. He cussed some, and I did too, and then we both scrambled up and chased after the big, hulking figure that was running out the front door.

"Stop!" yelled Bernie. "Help! Police!"

We busted out onto the night sidewalk, Bernie in the lead, still hollering, "Stop! Thief!" and it was a sight to remember, the way pedestrians scattered and heads ducked back inside open windows. There wasn't an ounce of help in a carload of them city folks.

But there *was* a squad car at the foot of the street, down on Riverside Drive, and the cop had just gotten out with a big stack of parking tickets in his hand. He looked up, and as Bernie yelled again, dropped the wad of tickets and hauled out his big old .38 Police Special.

He pointed it at the running mugger and yelled, "Halt! Hold it right there, or I'll shoot."

The mugger growled at the cop, "Is that all you got to do, chase us poah old black women?"

Bernie stared at the mugger's face and said, "I'll be a dirty son of a bitch."

My attacker was a woolly-haired, three-hundred-pound black woman.

EIGHT

Bernie and me had to go down to the precinct house to swear out a complaint, and from the way we got treated you'd have figured it was *us* who did the mugging. We both had to give our names and addresses and occupations, and when I said, "Actor," the cops all turned and looked at me like I was some kind of freak. But I sure in hell wasn't going to say "unemployed," not after the things Alice had been telling me.

Anyway, we answered all their questions, like how old were we, and had we ever been arrested before, and did we take drugs.

"Listen," I said to the cop who seemed to be in charge, "what are you asking *us* all the questions for?" I pointed at the big black woman. "Ask *her*. She's the one you arrested."

Quickly, the policeman said, "No, no, that's wrong. We haven't arrested anyone."

"What the hell do you mean, you ain't arrested her?

That big nigger woman jumped me and stole my money, didn't she? And you caught her dead to rights, didn't you?"

Sternly, the cop said, "Watch your tongue, mister. You can't use language like that in here."

"Language like what?"

"Like—like what you called the lady."

"Lady! She's a hugger-mugger! She purt near mashed my windpipe into Jello. Why don't you ask what *her* name is, and where *she* lives, and what *her* occupation is, other than mugging old men in elevators?"

"We can't do that," said the cop. "We'd be violating her rights."

"Then how come you're asking me all this stuff? What about *my* rights."

"You're not accused of anything, sir, so you don't *have* any rights."

I was so mad that I got to sucking in my breath and I couldn't seem to let any of it out, so I guess I kind of swelled up like a banty rooster on the make. All I could say was "Wuh! Wuh!"

The cop pulled back, alarmed. "What I meant," he said, "was that you don't have any *legal* rights. The right to remain silent, the right to consult an attorney——"

"Wuh!"

"The right to have an attorney appointed free of charge if you can't afford one——"

"Wuh!"

"*She* has those rights. But since you aren't accused of anything, we can ask you whatever we want."

"Wuh!"

"However, the lady *is* accused. So we can't even talk to her until her attorney arrives."

"Wuh—what a pile of shit!"

The cop leaned forward sternly. "I don't want to have to caution you again about your talk, mister. Abusive or obscene language uttered to an officer in the performance of his duty is a serious offense, and——"

"What about her?" I yelled.

"We'll question her as soon as her attorney gets here."

"And when do you expect that? Sometime around the vernal equinox?"

"He'll get here when he gets here. The attorneys who handle these needy cases are very busy and——"

"Needy! Who's the neediest? Her or me? She took all my money, remember?"

"Well, sir, that's something that will have to be decided by the judge. After all, it's your word against the lady's——"

"Some lady! How many times have you had her in here before?"

"I'm sorry, we aren't allowed to divulge——"

"But she's got my money. Four fifty-dollar bills and——"

"Can you identify them?"

"Hell, yes. They're printed green on one side and black on the other and there's a picture of Ulysses S. Grant——"

"I meant, do you have the serial numbers?"

I stared at him. "Officer, how much money do you have on you?"

He stared back. "Perhaps forty dollars."

"What's the serial numbers?"

He tightened his lips. "I don't have to know the serial numbers."

"Why not?"

"Because *I* haven't reported my money stolen."

Uneasily, Bernie shifted his feet. "Can I go?" he asked.

"No," said the cop.

"But I've told you everything I know."

The cop leaned forward. "You've told us everything you *want* us to know."

"He told you the truth," I said. "Not that you'd know what *that* is, even if it came up and bit you on the leg."

"I've cautioned you already," the cop began.

"Mistah *Po*-liceman," said a new voice.

We all turned and stared.

It was the big black woman.

"What do you want?" asked the cop.

"Is this when I cop me a plea, or do I got to wait for my lawyer man, or what?"

Sweating, the cop said, "Don't say anything until he gets here."

"What's the matter?" I asked. "Don't you want to hear the 'lady' admit she did it?"

"Don't you say a word, Mary Lou," said the cop.

"But my ass is *soah*," she said.

"It'll only be a few more minutes," pleaded the cop. "If you talk now, you'll ruin everything."

I got up and went over to the big black woman. "Lady, let's make a deal," I said. "Give me back my money and I'll drop the whole thing."

"Don't say a word, Mary Lou!" yelled the cop. "Any admission of guilt can and will be used against you in a court of law. Wait for your lawyer."

"Doan look like he *never* come," said Mary Lou. "Maybe I better do like the John say, 'cause I sure ain't going back to that jail no more, and that's the honest truth."

"Right on!" I said. I was pushing to get my money back. At that moment, I didn't really give a damn about anything else. Let somebody else worry about Mary Lou. "Give me back my money and I'll drop all charges."

"Charges?" bellowed a new, masculine voice. "*Charges*? Sergeant, I warn you, if my client has been deprived of her constitutional rights——"

"Deprived!" I yelled. "She's got more rights than Carter's got pills!"

"She hasn't said a thing, Mr. Michaelson," said the cop.

"Mary Lou," said the lawyer, "my name is Sid Michaelson, and you don't have a thing to worry about. The court has appointed me to represent indigent clients——"

"Indigent? What that, man?" asked Mary Lou.

"Without funds," said the lawyer.

"You mean, busted? No money?"

"That's right. But don't worry. The Law extends its protection to all, regardless of race, creed, color, or ability to pay."

"Shee-*it*!" said Mary Lou. "I doan want none of them chickenshit *free* defenses. I wants the best money can buy."

She shoved one huge, pink-nailed black fist into his face, clutching a wad of green paper.

"Here!" said Mary Lou. "Take these here four fifty-dollar bills!"

NINE

You ever hear of a postponement? That's when you, and all your witnesses, and the assistant district attorney they assigned to you, all show up at the courthouse and wait around for your case to be called, and then you find out that the attorney for the defense has gotten another postponement and nobody bothered to notify you about it.

"Well?" I asked Mr. Shaw, the young assistant district attorney. "Are they going to show up this time, or did that bastard Michaelson get another one of them postponements?"

We were there early, as usual. Alice and me had showed up a few minutes before ten. But Bernie wasn't here this time. After the last postponement, which was our third, he blew his cork.

"If I keep running down here and leaving my building alone, the tenants are going to complain to Mr. Churchill. They're just looking for an excuse to cause trouble for me anyway, because I won't make toilet repairs after ten at night."

Mr. Shaw pleaded with him to be patient. "That's part of Michaelson's strategy," he said. "It's standard in minor cases like this."

"What's so minor about getting your neck squoze and losing all your money?" I asked.

Mr. Shaw ignored me. "Sid wants you to get discouraged at all the delay. He's hoping that one day our witnesses won't show up, and then he'll move for a dismissal."

"That no-good bastard," I said.

"Don't say that," Mr. Shaw warned.

"Well, he *is* a no-good bastard. This is the fourth time he's had us down here."

"And he always waits until the last minute, to waste our time," Alice said. "Why does the judge let him get away with it?"

"The judge has to protect the defendant's rights," said Mr. Shaw.

"I got a craw full of hearing all about Mary Lou's rights," I said.

"Don't say that!"

"Say what?"

"Don't call her Mary Lou."

"Well, what in hell am I *supposed* to call her? If I call her a big nigger woman who mugged me, which is what she surely is, everybody gets upset, and——"

I stopped. Because, just like everybody else, now Mr. Shaw was upset, too.

With his eyes closed, he said, "You are *not* to call her that."

"Call her what?"

"What you said."

"All right," I told him. "Only that's why I started calling her Mary Lou."

"Don't call her that, either."

"But it's her *name*."

"You aren't supposed to know her name. You're not supposed to know anything about her. If you call her by name, Sid Michaelson can seize the opportunity to suggest there may have been previous connections between you and the defendant."

"Let me tell you something, Mr. Shaw. If your buddy Sid tries to make out I been hanky-panking with that big old black woman, I'll shove that goddamned leather briefcase right up his hairy ass until the handle sticks out his ears."

Alice touched my arm. "I know it's frustrating, all this time wasted, but those are the rules. If we follow them, we'll get justice eventually."

"If we don't get that there justice pretty soon, I may not live to enjoy it."

"Be patient, Fred."

Mr. Shaw looked like he wanted to applaud her. I just grunted.

The courtroom was filling up now. But no Bernie. It looked like he had meant it when he told us he wasn't going to waste no more time in court.

I couldn't really blame him. It seemed like I'd spent the last two weeks downtown, either waiting around in court for a postponement to be called, or telling my story over and over to Mr. Shaw.

If he asked me once, he asked me a hundred times

where I got the money Mary Lou stole, and every time
I told him about the Deep Balm commercials, he shook
his head sadly and said, "Sid'll cut us to pieces on that.
It just doesn't sound believable."

"What the hell does that matter? It's the truth, ain't
it? We can prove it, can't we?"

Mr. Shaw scratched his nose. "That's not the point,
Mr. Frederickson. Sid won't give us the chance to prove
anything. He'll tear at everything you say, nit-picking
little details you may have forgotten. He'll try to create
doubt in the mind of the court that an—ah—
unconventional gentleman such as yourself actually *had*
two hundred dollars. Before you can even produce your
tax records to substantiate your claim, he'll cut off the
subject to move on to some other area."

"Good for him," I said, "because I ain't got no tax records to show him anyhow."

Mr. Shaw stared at me. "Why not?"

"Never had no need for them."

Mr. Shaw looked away and groaned.

"Here comes the judge," Alice said. "And our star
witness, Bernie, is nowhere in sight."

Glumly, Mr. Shaw answered, "And here comes Sid
Michaelson with a big smile on his face. I think we're
in trouble."

"Oyez, oyez, all rise," said the clerk. "This court is
now in session."

We all stood, and then we all sat, and while our case
was being called, I stared across the room at Mary Lou,
and I couldn't believe what I saw. She had on a black
dress, and I guess it contained enough material to make

a good-sized tent, and she wore one of them lace veils like a Spanish nun, and so help me Hannah, she had her big old fingers working on the beads of a yard-long rosary attached to a wooden cross as long as a crowbar.

Mr. Shaw looked around once more in hopes of spotting Bernie. No luck. He got up and said, "If it please the court, the People request a postponement in order to locate a key witness."

Sid Michaelson jumped up. "I protest!" he yelled. "The Defense is here, ready and eager to present its case. This poor woman . . . this suffering mother . . . has stood in jeopardy through four appearances now. There has been delay enough. If the Prosecution is unable to present its case at this late date, I respectfully request this court to dismiss all charges and return this unfortunate woman to the bosom of her anxious family."

Mary Lou clicked her beads and mumbled, "Yas suh, praise be to God!"

Now I jumped up. "Just one pea picking minute! Any delays in this here trial, bub, has been because you wanted them on account of you hoped we'd get wore out sitting around waiting for you to finally get down to business. I thought you lawyers was supposed to stand up for law and order. But right now, you got my four fifty-dollar bills stuck in your pocket. You know what I think? I think you'n her are in cahoots!"

During this, I felt Alice pulling at one of my arms, and Mr. Shaw had hold of the other, but I was so hot mad that I couldn't really pay attention to anything but the words in my head that I was trying to say, although they wasn't exactly the words that were coming out. Everybody else was talking too, but I didn't really notice or hear them until my own motor run down. Then things got awful quiet.

That Michaelson feller commenced to sputtering like an old Ford tractor with the choke pulled out. "Outrage!" he shouted. "I demand a mistrial!"

The judge rapped with his big old wooden hammer, and things got quiet again. He leaned forward. "Mr. Prosecutor, will you explain this outburst?"

Poor Mr. Shaw, he looked ready to strangle on his own tongue, but he stood up like a man and said, "Your Honor, I apologize for Mr. Frederickson's behavior. This poor seventy-year-old man, robbed of his life's savings, simply lost control, and——"

"I object!" screamed Michaelson.

"Sustained," said the judge, a touch of weariness in his voice. "Perhaps we can cease and desist with the usual fireworks and get on with the day's work? The court has a heavy calendar this month. Suppose I entertain motions?"

"Motion to dismiss," Michaelson said quickly.

"Denied. Is the Prosecution prepared to put on its case?"

"Your Honor," said Shaw, "I had originally requested a postponement, and the court has yet to rule on that motion."

"Postponement denied," said the judge. "We can't tie up the docket indefinitely with this one minor case."

I jumped up again. "You give *them* three postponements, Judge Your Honor, and now you won't even give Mr. Shaw one? That don't seem hardly fair."

"Mr. Shaw," said the judge.

"Yes, Your Honor," said Mr. Shaw. He turned to me. "Mr. Frederickson, you've got to sit down and remain silent, or this court can find you in contempt."

I opened my mouth, but Alice grabbed my wrist and yanked me down in my chair. "Fred! Be *quiet*. You'll never get anything accomplished this way."

"Don't seem to me like we're getting much accomplished anyhow."

"Shh," she said. "The judge is talking."

". . . see no reason why two experienced trial lawyers like yourselves cannot arrive at a reasonable compromise that will both achieve the ends of Justice and still conserve the time of this court."

"Your Honor," said Sid Michaelson. "May Counsel approach the bench?"

"What the hell's going on?" I asked Alice.

"It's just like Perry Mason," she said. "I think they're going to agree on a plea."

"What the hell do you mean, agree on a plea? She done it, didn't she? What is there to agree on?"

Up by the judge's bench, old Michaelson and Shaw were bobbing and dipping their heads like two speckled chicken neck-deep in the feed box. Michaelson would say something, and Shaw would back off and shake his head, and then *he'd* move in and make a counteroffer, and it would be Michaelson's time to back off shaking his own head.

Finally, they all seemed to arrive at an agreement, because they both nodded and spoke to the judge, who nodded too, and then they all split up and Mr. Shaw came back to our table wearing a big grin.

"Not bad," he said. "They're going to cop a plea."

"What does that mean?" I asked.

"She's going to plead guilty," said Alice. "See, Fred? I told you if you'd only be patient——"

"Well, it's not exactly that simple," said Mr. Shaw. "Sid correctly probed the weakness in our case because of our not having Bernie present as a corroborating witness——"

"I don't know rightly what you're saying," I told him, "but I got an idea it ain't good."

Flatly, Mr. Shaw said, "They'll plead guilty to the reduced charge of simple assault."

"Assault! She goddamned near killed me. Ain't that attempted murder? She stole all my money. Ain't that grand larceny or something? How the hell can she get off with simple assault?"

"Because," Shaw said patiently, "we simply cannot prove those other allegations. We're lucky, to tell the truth, to get a guilty plea on the lesser charge. Sid as much as hinted to me that if we'd actually come to trial, his counterstrategy would have been to involve Mr. Frederickson himself in an assault complaint."

I started to get up. "I am going to rearrange that gentleman's face for him."

"Be *still*!" Alice yanked me back into my seat. "Mr. Shaw, what does that mean? Pleading guilty to simple assault?"

"Well, it could go as high as ninety days."

"That ain't much," I said, simmering down. "But at least it'll keep her from mashing some other feller's windpipe for a spell."

"Of course," Mr. Shaw went on, "the judge will probably suspend the sentence and put her on probation."

"He'll *what*?"

Before Mr. Shaw could answer, the judge banged his gavel down and said, "Mary Lou Pelham, please stand."

Still working at her beads, Mary Lou got up just like butter wouldn't melt in her mouth. She was sweet old Aunt Jemima, dragged away from frying her latest stack of flapjacks for the hungry field hands. Looking at her, you'd never guess she had almost killed me in that dark lobby. "Yes suh, Judge," she said.

"Mary Lou," said the judge, "do you understand the charges that have been brought against you?"

"I shoah do," she said loudly. "That dried-up old honky over there done gambled away all his money, or maybe he never had none, so he——"

Sid Michaelson whispered something to her, and Mary Lou's face screwed up as she tried to concentrate. "Oh," she said. *"Oh!"*

"Your Honor," Michaelson said smoothly, "my client misunderstood your question. She thought she was being called upon to defend herself."

"No, Mary Lou," the judge said patiently. "Now, please listen carefully and try to understand. The original charges of aggravated assault and grand larceny have been dropped. Your attorney has indicated a willingness to enter a plea of guilty to simple assault, and the People, that is, the State, have agreed to accept this plea. Do you understand?"

"I shoah do," Mary Lou said, grinning and rattling her beads. "Mr. Michaelson, here, he done copped a plea."

The judge winced, but he went on gamely. "Now, I

want you to understand that no 'deal' has been made with this court. If you plead guilty to this lesser charge, you *could* still be sent to jail——"

Mary Lou reacted like she'd been bitten by a snake. "No, sir!" she said. "I ain't going to no jail. I done *been* there, and I ain't going back *no* more."

"Now, Mary Lou," said the judge, "I didn't say you *had* to go to jail. I merely said that you *might*——"

"I heard what you said, Judge, and I ain't going. No way. Them jails is dirty, and they doan feed you good, and all them butch dykes want to do is gobble yoah pussy——"

Helplessly, the judge looked to Sid Michaelson, who dragged Mary Lou over into a corner and really chewed her out in a harsh whisper we could hear all the way across the courtroom.

"*Shut up!*" he told her. "The judge is on your side. He wants to help you. But you've got to play along. Now, tell him you're guilty and throw yourself on the mercy of the court."

Mary Lou rolled the whites of her eyes. She nodded. She was really scared now. I could see she was playing the parts of two different people. One was Old Lady Handkerchief-Head, giving the judge an excuse to go easy on her. The other one slipped angry black glances toward me. The other was the one I'd met in the lobby.

Sid Michaelson led her down in front of the judge's bench and Mary Lou wailed, "I *done* it, Your Honor Judge!"

"Very well," said the judge. "Now, it is the decision of this court——"

Mary Lou's voice shook the walls. "I throws myself on the mercy of this here court!"

The judge's face was like a big red balloon, ready to explode. He gripped the edge of the bench with both hands and said quickly, "to sentence you to ninety days, sentence to be suspended and prisoner placed on probation. Mary Lou, do you know what that means?"

Slowly, she said, "I doan got to go to jail?"

"Not if you behave yourself. We are giving you another chance, Mary Lou. Mr. Michaelson will explain the probation procedure to you. I might add, he provided you with an able defense. You owe him a great deal."

Her eyes flashing like an angry cat's, Mary Lou said, "I doan owe him *nuthin'*! I paid that man good."

The judge sighed. "Case dismissed."

As everyone filed out, I mumbled, "What the hell happened? He let her *off*?"

Mr. Shaw and Sid Michaelson shook hands. Michaelson said, "Hey, Bunkie, how's the wife?"

"Who knows?" said Mr. Shaw. "She divorced me last July."

"Oh," said Michaelson. "Well, cheer up. You can't win them all."

Alice and me, we found ourselves alone in the long hall with its dark green stripes painted waist high and signs reading "Superior Court, Part III."

Numbly, Alice said, "I don't believe it. She didn't even know what was happening, but she got off anyway."

"I told you before," I said. "But you wouldn't listen.

The Law don't look out for nobody but the lawyers."

Mary Lou come out by herself. She had wadded up the rosary beads and stuck them in her purse, but the wooden cross still hung out.

She stared across the hall at us. Her eyes narrowed in her fat, black face, and there wasn't anything funny about her any more as she said, "White man, you done made me spend my four fifty-dollar bills to keep out of the jailhouse, and I ain't going to forget it. You better watch yoah step, 'cause I gonna *get* you."

TEN

Well, as you might expect, those developments in court shook Alice and me up a mite. So we took some of that Deep Balm money and went upstate, to them Catskill Mountains. I told Alice it was just a little weekend vacation, but I had something else on my mind.

The bus ride was nice, once we got out of the city, which didn't take long because we drove into one of them long tunnels right after we got out of the terminal. The destination sign on the front of the bus said, "Binghamton," but the driver promised he'd let us off at Roscoe, New York.

"I never even heard of Roscoe," Alice said. "Where is it? *What* is it?"

"Search me," I said. "I told Bernie we wanted to get out of town and sit under the trees, and maybe look at some deer or catch some fish, and he said Roscoe is the ticket. So I had telephone information get me the number of a hotel up there, and I called them, and they said, come on up. They're expecting us in time for dinner."

"Fred," Alice said softly. "You're awfully nice."

"I ain't no such thing," I said. "I'm mean and cantankerous and I got to have my own curmudgeonly way."

"I *like* your way."

"Quiet, big woman."

The rows and rows of suburban houses dropped behind us as we passed a big hill that had some flat brown buildings perched on it, above a sign that read, "Motel on the Mountain," and then the bus was driving through steep hills, and some of them had little patches of snow where it was shady.

"If there's snow here already," I said, "it's sure flying by now in Wyoming."

Alice stared out the window. "Are you sorry you stayed?"

I took out a pint of Old GrandDad I'd bought at a liquor store in the bus terminal and took a deep swig. "Now where do you get ideas like that, Alice? We got us a nice warm place to live and a color TV set to look at. We grabbed us more money for less work than anything I know of short of maybe bank robbing. And we're housing together, which I'm fast to admit is the nicest, sweetest thing that's happened to me in a month of Sundays."

Alice's eyes misted up and she pressed her cheek against the cold, frosty window. Outside, big pine trees rushed past.

"I'm sorry, Fred," she whispered.

"What's there to be sorry for? Here, have a taste. This is real sippin' whiskey."

She choked down a little swallow and handed the bottle back. "It's just—this mess. That awful woman. Oh, Fred, she got away with *everything.*"

"We ain't finished yet, her'n me," I said. "A woman like that, she's got a long memory. By now, in her mind, it's me that hurt *her,* not the other way around. I ain't going to rest easy while she's still walking around."

Alice made a frightened animal sound. "Oh, Fred, don't say that."

"Honey, all I'm saying is that big old nigger woman told me she was going to *get* me, and I truly believe she's going to try."

Alice pressed the knuckles of one hand against her mouth. "But what will we do? We can't count on the police, I know that now."

"At least you're learning." I punched her a gentle tonk on the arm. "Come on there, Miss Alice. Where's your gumption?"

Slowly, she shook her head. "I guess it sort of leaked out of me during these last few days."

"Well, honey, don't you fret none. That big black gal may try, but she don't *get* Fred that easy. This time I'm going to be watching out for her. She ain't going to sneak up on me outside no elevator anymore."

Alice took the bottle from me and drank. "You were right after all," she said softly. "Nobody's looking out for us, nobody's going to keep them from breaking down the doors and taking what they want. . . ."

"Wrong," I said. "I told you nobody *else* is going to do it. But, baby, *we* sure in hell are. They ain't going to catch us in the same bind twice running."

Plaintively, she said, "I don't *want* to!"

"You don't want to what?"

"I don't want to be *in* this. I don't have anything to prove. All I want is to be left alone."

"That's your privilege, Alice," I said. "I didn't take you to raise. If you don't like the ride, why just get off. I ain't got no hooks in you."

"Oh, you fool," she said. She stopped, and stared down silently at her clenched hands. "I can't get off. I love you, Fred."

"No you don't, honey. You're just miserable and disillusioned with everything right now, and you've got a real bad case of the lonelies. You'll get over it."

"Don't try to flimflam me, you crusty old crock!" she said, with a spark of the old temper. "And don't get so uptight. I'm not staking any claims on your worthless carcass. But I'm worried about you. And do I need a license for *that*?"

"That's my girl," I said. "And I'm just as pleased to hear you say it. But you got to remember, I'm seventy years old, so don't go getting any long-range ideas, because they just ain't in the cards."

"You'll outlive most of us. You're too damned *mean* to die."

"Alice," I said, stroking her hair, "you got to take it one day at a time, and you don't even get no guarantee for *that*."

She turned away. "I know. But I don't like to think about it."

"Don't," I said. "Not today. Let's drink us some whiskey and enjoy ourselves, and let tomorrow take care of itself."

So we did, and when the bus let us off at Roscoe, we had a friendly glow on. I located the Antrim Lodge, and we checked in downstairs at the bar. The tall feller there, he give us a funny look when I said, "One room. One bed." But he didn't say nothing.

Alice followed me up the stairs, giggling.

"Hush that cackling, woman," I told her.

"Oh, Fred, I just can't help it. We scandalized that poor man. Here's me, six feet tall. And you, old as the hills. What he must *think*! All we need is a dwarf and a trained pony, and we're in business."

"Big gal, you got a dirty mind."

She giggled again and goosed me when I bent over to fit the key into the lock.

"Now, *stop* that, Alice."

But she didn't, so I pulled the door open and shoved her inside. She let out a little shriek and sprawled over the big double bed. I locked the door behind me.

Moving toward her, I said, "You brung this on yourself."

"I know, Fred," she said, and her eyes were deep and soft.

There wasn't much to this town of Roscoe. We walked through it in four or five minutes. They had one movie theater, and a supermarket, and a couple of sporting-goods stores with fishing gear in the windows, and Green's Garage, and that was just about it. We stopped in at a little bar called the Bow and Arrow and drank us a couple of cold Utica Club beers and talked to the nice little lady who runs the place.

"We're sort of tourist folks," I said. "Just taking it easy, but I hoped maybe I could show this big woman a couple of wild deer. Is that possible this time of year?"

"No reason why not," said the lady. "They've been herding up in the apple trees. Season's not open yet, so they're not too skitterish. They're early this year. They don't usually come down into the orchards until the fallen apples have frozen and fermented."

"You sound like you've been up there," I said.

She grinned. "I get my buck every year."

"I just bet you do, and with one shot, too. Which way do we go to this orchard?"

She examined me. "Can you climb a hill? A good steep one?"

"I reckon I got one more left in me."

That good old gal, she busted out laughing. "I asked for that one, I suppose, you old buzzard. Where are you folks from, anyway?"

"Kansas. My woman here's from Ohio. But we're both living down in New York City right now, for what little that's worth."

The lady started to say, "Your woman?" surprised-like, but she saw the grim "What do you want to make of it?" expression that come over Alice's face. She smiled and said, "Well, I wish you both luck. Not that you're likely to need it. You look happy as a pair of bees in the honeycomb right now."

"Thank you, ma'am," I said. "Now, where's this big old hill you mentioned?"

She pointed. "Go down this road to where the stream crosses under it, and turn right, up along the stream bed. Keep going, right over the top, and you'll find a little valley full of apple trees. If you hurry, you'll make it before sundown. That's when they usually start coming out."

"Let us have a six-pack," I said, "and we'll be on our way."

Alice carried the beer in a paper bag as I led the way, up alongside the stream that churned and frothed at our feet. The woods were damp and cool, and it was good to feel the rotted leaves under my feet after those hard, barren sidewalks down in the city.

"Slow down, old man," Alice puffed. "This isn't supposed to be a race."

"You're out of condition, big woman," I said, but I slacked off a mite. We had plenty of time. The sun was still high, painting dapples of yellow and red over the fallen leaves.

We crested the hill, and the valley spread out beneath us. It was a little tree-locked hollow, choked with apple trees gone back to the wild. I tasted the wind, and it was blowing straight across the valley into our faces, so I pointed at a fallen log and said, "We might as well sit here for a spell."

Alice popped open two of the cans and we sipped the cold beer and got our breaths back.

"Can we talk?" she whispered.

"If we hold it down. The wind's blowing our way, so it'll carry the sound away from them. If they come."

"Oh, I hope they do!"

"Well, either they will or they won't. No sense in worrying. Anyway, this ain't the last chance you'll ever have to see a deer."

"I know . . . but I have this funny feeling that if we don't see them now, we never will."

"Don't pay feelings like that no mind at all," I said. "You can't depend on nothing except what actually happens. All the rest is bullshit."

"*Fred!*"

"What's the matter, big woman? You never heard the word before?"

"Of course I've *heard* it. But it's just—wrong, here."

The dying sun washed across her face, and I could see its golden glow through the light peach fuzz on her cheeks. I reached over and touched her.

"You are absolutely right, Miss Alice, and I apologize."

She gave my fingers a little pecking kiss and I yanked them back. She laughed.

"Don't worry, Fred. I won't eat you. Yet."

"Miss Alice, you got a dirty, *dirty* mind."

She started to answer, and just then she saw something down below us, because the words caught in her throat and, instead, she pointed. I leaned over to look.

Fifty yards down the hill, a large reddish-brown doe had just stepped out into a patch of sunlight. Her ears were pointed straight up, and she was sniffing the air, but I knew she couldn't hear or smell us. I motioned for Alice to be still.

There came another blur of motion and now two speckled fawns stood beside the doe.

"Two!" Alice whispered. "Oh, look at the little babies."

"The does mostly always drop twins," I said. "They're feeding on those fallen apples."

"They're so cute," she breathed.

"Just hold real still," I warned. "I bet you anything there's a buck hanging back there somewheres. That big old buck, he won't come out of the trees until he's sure everything's nice and safe."

"Just like a man," Alice said. I pinched her thigh. She hissed and winced, but she held real still so's she wouldn't startle the deer.

"Here he comes," I said softly. Alice gripped my hand.

The buck didn't step or jump out into the clearing. He simply *appeared*. One second he wasn't there, and in the next blink of an eye he *was*.

He was a big golden-brown ten-point. I heard Alice suck in her breath as she saw him.

"Oh, Fred . . . he's beautiful!"

"Shhh."

The buck moved further out into the clearing. His alert eyes seemed to be fixed directly on us. Alice's fingers tightened on my hand. Then he looked away, bent his head, and commenced to grazing on the fallen apples.

There came more movement, brown and silken, and

117

now there were at least a dozen deer in the clearing, munching the apples and frolicking with each other in mock battle.

I whispered to Alice, "The bucks herd up and play together this time of the year. But later on, when they're in the rut, they'll rattle horns over these same does."

Two button-horn bucks, with antlers that weren't more than the length of a cigarette, pawed the ground and pretended to do battle. One slipped and fell, and there was such a look of surprise on his face that Alice laughed out loud. At once, all the deer in the clearing froze, ears twitching.

"Don't move," I said, real low.

The first big buck sniffed the air, turning his head first one way and then the other. None of the other animals moved. Finally, he lowered his head and started eating again.

"Nope," I said. "These deer ain't been shot at yet. They're too happy. If somebody'd been jacking them, they'd be a lot more nervous."

The sun sank lower and the shadows poked long, moving shapes across the little clearing. We sat there until it was so dark that all we could see of the deer were the white flags of their tails, flicking in the air as they grazed peacefully in the abandoned apple orchard.

We snuck back down the hill quietly, so's not to spook the herd, and when we reached the road, Alice wrapped both arms around my neck and hugged me until I heard my bones crack.

"Hey, there!" I yelled. "Don't *kill* me!"

"Oh, Fred!" she said. "Thank you. I'll never forget them. They were so beautiful. You were right. It gives you a *good* feeling, watching them."

"You try and hang onto that feeling, girl," I said. "It don't come along none too often."

ELEVEN

Next morning, after breakfast, I left Alice talking with that good old gal in the Bow and Arrow, and I took me a walk down the road away from town to a little gun-smith's shop I'd noticed. It wasn't much, just one room in the front of a garage.

A little bell hooked to the front door jangled and brought the owner out of the back.

"Morning," says he. "What can I do for you?"

"I need me a little gun for a lady," I said. "Say a .25, or at most a .32 automatic."

"I've got a seven-shot .32," he said. "Italian parts, but it was assembled in this country. One of the last ones we got, before that new law was passed."

"One of them Saturday Night Specials?"

That made him mad. "I don't stock junk," he said. "This is a fine little weapon. Yes, it had to be assembled here, because of the gun control laws about importing pistols. But it's quality workmanship. And it fills a sporting purpose, in addition to defense."

"Calm down," I said. "Both of us know what that little baby is for. It's for shooting folks in the belly at ranges up to ten feet and no more. There ain't a speck of sporting purpose anywhere in that kind of gun. It's strictly for self-defense, and that's fine, because that's exactly what I'm looking for."

That softened him down a little. "What's wrong with that?" he asked. "A man's got a right to defend himself, hasn't he?"

"My sentiments exactly," I said.

He put the flat, pearl-handled automatic out on the counter for me to look at. I ejected the clip and pulled the slide back to be sure the chamber was empty. I hefted it. It balanced nice. I shoved the clip back in with my thumb.

"I'll take it," I said.

"Fine," he said. "May I see your permit?"

I put three fifty-dollar bills on the counter. "Right there is my permit."

His Adam's apple bobbed. "I'm sorry, sir, the law——"

"My friend, if you think I'm the *po*-lice, you must be hard of seeing. As far as I'm concerned, this little deal is strictly between you and me, private."

His eyes flicked to the door, the window, back to me, and then he smiled. "Mister," he said, "I thought I had a little .32 automatic to show you, but it seems to be missing. I left that window wide open last night, and I bet somebody got in and stole it."

He turned his back on me, went over and made a big

deal out of shutting the window. When he came back, the gun was tucked out of sight in my pocket.

I nodded at the money on the counter. "You better lock your money up, too," I said. "You don't want to leave cash lying around here on the counter. It might blow away."

He closed his fingers over the bills. "Thanks. Say, you wouldn't need a couple of boxes of .32 pistol shells, would you? I don't have any more use for them."

"Might as well take them off your hands," I said. "Never know when I might run into a gun they'd fit."

He put them in a bag, two boxes of fifty shells each. "Ten dollars'll do it," he said.

I busted out laughing and tossed him the ten. "Here. What did you do for work before you got into this business? Stick up liquor stores?"

Without smiling, he said, "I sold used cars."

I picked Alice up back at the Bow and Arrow. We got another six-pack of beer and went up the hill and sat in the shade.

"I got a little present for you," I told her. "That's why I really brung you up here. I know you ain't going to like it, but I want you to take it anyway, and then I'm going to teach you how to use it."

I handed her the flat little box. She looked at it. "I don't understand."

"Open it up."

She did, and shrank back. "Fred! It's a *gun!*"

"Don't worry. It ain't loaded."

"Ugh! Take it away."

"No, ma'am." I picked it up and snapped back the slide. "This here is a .32 automatic pistol, Alice, and by itself, it ain't nothing but cold metal and plastic. By itself, it can't hurt a fly."

"But I don't want a *gun!*"

"Alice," I said patiently, "you may have been born in Ohio, but you're sure as hell a city gal now. You city people just don't understand about guns. When you see one, you pull back like you touched a spider. 'Oh, a *gun!*' What's wrong with a gun?"

"Guns kill people."

"*People* kill people. Sometimes they use a gun. Sometimes they use a knife. Sometimes they use a car. A hell of a lot more people get killed with cars than with guns, but you don't hear nobody wailing, 'Oh, a *car!*' "

"But we need cars. They're useful."

"Big woman, I hope the time never comes for you to find out, but sometimes guns can be mighty useful too."

"Please, Fred, let's not argue. I know you think you're doing what's best. But I just don't want anything to do with this—this thing." She slid the little automatic off her lap into the grass.

I stood up. "In that case, Missy, I'm sorry to say goodbye."

I started down the hill. She called after me, "Fred! Where are you going?"

"Wyoming."

"But you *can't!*"

"You just watch me."

"But why? What have I done?"

"Alice, honey, I told you I was going sooner or later. I reckon it's got to be sooner than later."

"Just because I don't want a gun? That's insane!"

"That ain't the only reason, but it's part of it. Alice, in spite of everything that's happened, you still won't admit to yourself that you got to stand up and watch out for your own protection, because there ain't nobody else going to do it. You say the words, but you don't really believe them. I can't be around all the time to watch out after you. Now what are you going to do if that big nigger woman comes after me, and I ain't there? She's just as likely to bust you in half out of plain meanness. Before I'll see that happen, I intend to light out of these parts."

"I wouldn't let her in. If I saw her on the street, I'd run."

"You wouldn't get the chance. No, big woman, I won't be held responsible."

Her lips tightened. "All right, go. This is silly anyway. It was only that I felt sorry for you. . . ."

She stopped. She was too decent to let it end on a lie.

I bent over and kissed her forehead. "You be good now, Miss Alice, y'hear?"

She grabbed my hand and held it pressed against her cheek, which was all wet. "Don't go, Fred, please. I'm sorry, I'll do what you want. I promise."

"Are you sure, baby? You got to do it because you think it's right, not because you're doing what I *made* you do."

125

She drew me down beside her on a fallen log. "I'm so mixed up," she said. "I guess I know you're right. But it goes against everything I've been taught."

"There ain't nothing wrong with the things you been taught. That's the way things ought to be. But don't ever make the mistake of mixing up what ought to be and what *is*. There's evil out there, hon, and it comes in all sizes and colors. Now, the people who run The Law, they somehow got the evil all mixed up with the good, and they treat both the same. There ain't nothing evil about a hammer if you use it to drive nails. But if you bash in somebody's head with it, or smash open a window . . . well, it's the same way for a gun. You can use one for murder. Or you can protect yourself with it. But these days, The Law don't hold no more with anyone protecting himself. According to them, if you've got a gun, you mean to do evil with it. Now that doesn't follow. Still, we might be able to live with what they want us to do, if they'd only protect us themselves. They've got a lot of rules on the books, and the honest folks obey them, and the crooks, they just laugh like hell and go get their guns they got stashed illegally."

"But that's what the law's for, to keep them from having weapons, and to protect us."

"No, ma'am. The Law'll keep an honest man from having a gun, because *he* obeys the law. But them others don't. And The Law don't protect you, not really. It operates on the principle of punishment, not prevention. It won't prevent some character from poking a knife into you, although if they get lucky, the cops might track him down and stash him in the hoosegow. But what does that mean these days? There ain't no death penalty. He'll be out in a few years, and meanwhile *you'll* be dead forever and ever. That ain't what I'd consider a fair swop. That's why I bought you this here pistol, to even up the odds a little."

"But it seems so . . . brutal and cynical."

"It is that, I suppose. But what else can you be unless you just want to gamble that you'll be lucky and Mary Lou or nobody else'll ever come after you?"

"All right," she said tightly. "What do you want me to do?"

"Go get that gun from where you threw it. And bring the beer, too. We'll do us some target practice."

She searched in the grass and found the little .32. Holding it gingerly, she picked up the bag of beer and came back down to the log.

"Ah," I said, sipping one of the Utica Clubs. "You can have one too, as soon as you finish your first three lessons. Lesson Number One. This is the safety, this little catch. When it's shoved over here, it locks the trigger in place and you can't shoot. Point it at the stump and try."

Trembling, she said, "It's not loaded?"

"Nope, I cleaned her out. Now, hold it just like you're pointing your finger. Open your eyes! How the hell do you expect to see what you're doing?"

Still shaking, she more or less aimed the gun and flinched violently as she tried to pull the trigger.

"Fine," I said. "That's Lesson Number One. The safety. Always make sure it's on until you're actually ready to fire. That way, you won't shoot yourself in the foot by accident if you drop your purse."

Still aiming, she said, "It doesn't want to stay where I point it."

"That's because you're all tensed up yanking at that locked-down trigger. Slip the safety off—just push it over to the left. That's right. Now, dry-fire a couple of times to get the feel of the trigger squeeze. Don't worry, it's not loaded."

Alice kept closing her eyes and forcing them open again as she took up the trigger slack.

"It doesn't want to go click," she said, and just then the hammer fell, and the gun went "POW!" and flew out of her hand. She shrieked and leaped back.

"Fred! What happened?"

I picked up the pistol and studied the stump she had been aiming at. "I think you missed," I said.

"But you said it wasn't loaded!"

"That's Lesson Number Two. Never trust *any*one, and that includes me, about a gun being empty."

"You fink! I believed you."

I ruffled her hair. "I know you did, and it was a dirty trick. But I bet you'll never forget it, and that's good. Now you'll act like a gun's loaded until you *know* it's empty." I slid the clip out. "Like this. *Now* it's empty. See? Here's the clip, and these are the bullets."

Nervously, she examined the little bronze-tipped shells. "They're not very big."

"Big enough," I said. "They'll take a man down and keep him there. Now, really hold her in there and prac-

128

tice squeezing that old trigger. Keep your eyes open this time. Just look straight down the barrel and put the front sight right in the middle of your target. Close your whole hand, real slow, just like you was squeezing a lemon."

She did, and the gun bucked in her hand again and went "POW!" This time she held onto it, but her face went red.

"You dirty bastard!" she yelled. "You did it to me again!"

"I sure did," I said, popping her a beer. "And that's Lesson Number Three. Always check the chamber, even if the clip's out. Just pull back the slide. If there's a shell hid in there, it'll eject."

"I'll never trust you again as long as I live," she said. But she took the beer.

I slipped two more shells into the clip, filling it. "Now, you already know all you really *have* to know," I told her. "One. Keep the safety on until you're ready to shoot. Two. Never trust anybody who tells you a gun's empty. Three. Always check the chamber."

She inhaled about half of the beer. "I want to try that again."

"Good girl. But first, let me show you something about shooting a handgun like this one. You don't have to worry about accuracy, because it ain't got none. What you do is get up as close as you can to your target . . ." and I walked up within spitting distance of the stump, "and let him have it."

I pulled off all seven shots as fast as I could squeeze

the trigger. The bark splintered and whirled up into the air, and seven bright yellow patches appeared in the wood.

The shots echoed in the woods and rang in our ears for a long, long time. I reloaded the clip, shoved it back into the automatic, and operated the slide to charge the chamber.

"You hit the stump the first shot," Alice said. "Why did you keep on shooting?"

"Because that's what I want you to do. Don't depend on one shot. You got seven, use them all. Set yourself a distance, say four or five feet away, and if somebody's coming at you, don't let him get one inch closer. Not one inch! I seen people let someone walk right up and take the goddamned gun out of their hand! Do that and you're dead. And once you start shooting, *keep* shooting. Empty it, and stick in the extra clip and empty *it* too. You ain't playing games. The idea is to take him out, so take him *out*."

"But I wouldn't want to *kill* anyone, Fred. All I want to do is stop him."

"Wrong. If you're going to shoot at all, shoot to kill, and make sure you *do* kill. Empty that goddamned clip."

"But what if I do and he's still coming?"

"Baby, that's when you run like hell."

I handed her the gun. She advanced slowly toward the stump. It was cool on the hill, but sweat stood out on her upper lip.

She lifted the little gun and fired.

Seven times.

Distantly, a crow cawed in sudden fright.

The echoes bounced off the hills. Then they rolled to a stop.

I went over and examined the neat new ring of seven bright yellow holes she had put in the stump.

"Baby," I said, "You wouldn't have had to worry about this one anymore. *He* sure in hell wouldn't have kept coming at you."

TWELVE

It still don't sound too bad, does it? I mean, what's wrong with a girl defending herself?

Well, I swear, that's all I had im mind, in spite of the way it turned out. I don't know what you think about it, and. . . . No, that ain't so. I'm just poor-mouthing. I *know* what you think. Inside, you're all shaky and mad, because you're afraid of me and people like me. Well, that's all right. The truth is, there ain't no way for city people like you and woods people like me to exist side by side. We always get in each other's ways. So naturally, your kind has set out to get rid of my kind, and you're doing a mighty fine job of it, too.

You come tromping through the woods, scattering litter and waving guns around you've just bought and don't even know how to use. To get a payback on your investment of a couple of days, you gang up on some frightened doe and kill her out of season so your trip won't be wasted. You park your shiny new cars in our

front yards and cut through our fields without even saying "howdy-do." You chase our kids out of their own
swimming hole because you want to catch *your* fish.

Oh, you got money enough. Your car is a mile long.
Your hunting clothes are right out of *Field & Stream*.
You got it all. Everything but time. You went and
traded all those weeks and months and years of your
life for money. Now you'd like to buy a little dab back.

But you can't hire the fish to bite on that one afternoon a month that you can spare from making money.
You can't pay the partridge to bunch up and wait for
your big three-day-weekend hunt. You can't rent a
bright, sunny day when the weatherman decides it
ought to rain.

Those things take time, lots of it. They take gentle
waiting to come true. You can't hurry through the
woods with a time clock and track down anything but
disappointment.

How about that? I started out here mad as a hoot
owl, and all of a sudden I'm feeling sorry for you.

Alice and me, we got back to the big city after three
days up there at Roscoe, and we was like two new people. She even got herself a little tanned, and we'd
caught a nice mess of pan fish, crappies and bluegills,
which we put in a cooler packed in ice and brought
back for Bernie. Alice fired up those two boxes of shells
until she wasn't scared of the gun anymore. I bought
another two boxes of ammo and an extra clip for her to
carry in her purse, and for the first time since Mary
Lou made her threat, my mind rested easier.

I had tried to fool Alice a couple of times by sneaking a live round into the chamber when she wasn't looking, but she never got suckered again.

And she was a born marksman. Before that first day was out, she was firing a seven-shot group you could cover with your hand, and that's good pistol shooting in any man's language.

It wasn't necessary, but I warned her anyway: "That ain't no toy you got there, Alice. You don't haul it out to show off, or to try and scare people. When you take it out, it's on account of you got to shoot somebody."

"I know, Fred. Don't worry."

So I didn't. I put it clean out of my mind and we drove back to town and gave Bernie his fish.

Now that Alice seemed to have gotten hold of herself, housing with her was real comfortable. She bought herself some proper clothes, and got her hair done. Every morning she took off to "make the rounds," as she called it. And it paid off for her, too. She started getting parts in them TV commercials again, and pretty soon she had enough cash of her own so that she started talking about paying me back the money I'd spent on her.

"There ain't nothing to pay back," I told her. "If I needed money, I'd ask you for it, and no hesitation. But I don't. I got so much coming in now that I don't know where to bury it all."

And that was no lie. The Deep Balm people were so happy with the way things was going that they had me come back for another two days of commercials, and the ones I'd made that first time were running on all the

TV stations, and the cash just *rolled* in. It got so I couldn't walk down the street without somebody coming up to me, laughing, and asking, "Hey there, Chief Whitecloud, where's yore hoss?"

Yes, things was going good, and I guess I got a little fat and lazy. But you can't always foresee everything, and that's the truth.

We'd gone out to eat at one of them Chinese restaurants on Broadway, and then we stopped at the corner and had a couple of beers, so it was maybe ten o'clock at night when we got back upstairs to the apartment. The hall light was out, and that should have set off the alarm bells in my head, but like I said, those weeks of easy living must have slowed my brain down, because I didn't even pay it no mind. Like any fool, I stuck the key in the lock, saying, "You know, Alice, I think I'm getting used to that Chinese food——" and then the door busted open and I got hit in the head with a suitcase that split open, and radios and silverware and costume jewelry rained all over me.

I yelled, "Alice, *run!*" and then somebody run over *me.* I went down on my knees, and he finished the job by kicking me in the forehead and tromping on my gut as he went past. He was a big buck nigger in a flapping plaid sport shirt, and as he headed for the stairs, he yelled over his shoulder, "Come *on!*"

I was so busy gasping for air that I didn't see him go, just heard the hall door slam. Alice was trying to help me up as I found my voice and choked, "Don't go in . . . there's somebody else there. . . ."

Then Alice shrieked and backed away from me.

136

The woman had come out of the lighted apartment into the gloom of the hall. A butcher knife was shining like a streak of white lightning in her hand.

"I been looking for you, old man. Where'd you hide my money?"

Unable to move, I stared at Mary Lou Pelham. "Alice . . . run . . . call . . . police. . . ."

Mary Lou laughed. "Ain't no *po*-lice getting here in time to help *you*. Now, you just tell me where you got that money hid, old man."

I tried to stand up, but my gut hurt so bad that I couldn't get off my knees. Mary Lou laughed again, and it was enough to raise the hairs on the back of your neck.

"Pore ole man," she said. "You all busted up. Mary Lou'll do you a favor, put you outa yore misery."

"You won't find the money that way," said Alice, her voice trembling.

"Wait'll I get yore granpappy sliced up some, honey," said Mary Lou. "Den *you'll* tell me where it's at."

Alice stood dead still, and her voice was low. "You leave him alone."

Mary Lou bent over. "Tell ole man *good*bye."

I gathered my strength to try and grab the knife when she made her move, but the pain still had me bent over.

Alice's voice said, "Don't go near him."

"Shee-*it!*" said Mary Lou. "What you think you gone do with that little popgun? You put that thing away before I takes an' shoves it up yore twat."

"I mean it," said Alice. "Don't take another step.

137

You're close enough. Get out of here and leave us alone."

"Baby, you go fuck yo'self," said Mary Lou, and I saw the silver flash of the knife arcing down toward my throat. I threw up my arms, but I knew it was too late.

The little gun went ".POW!" and Mary Lou was on me, and I tried to roll away from her, and I felt sharp pain, and I could still hear the automatic going "POW! POW!"

Then there was silence. And a heavy weight on top of me. It shifted, moved, lightened, fell away.

Dimly, I saw Mary Lou stand up and back off. She had both hands clasped over her mountainous belly.

I tried to move, and felt dizzy. Something hot was running down my neck.

In a tiny voice Mary Lou said, "Why, gal, you done *shot* me. You *kilt* me. Why'd you want to do a thing like that for?" Her fingers scratched in the bloody folds of her dress. "Why'd you want to hurt Mary Lou?"

Alice screamed, "Because I *hate* you, you goddamned animal!"

Mary Lou's eyes widened. "I ain't never done nothing to you, why'd you want to go and kill me——"

Before Alice could answer, the big black woman relaxed suddenly. She slid down the wall and sat, spread-legged, with her skirt hiked up around her waist and the cloudy, dull glaze of death forming over her staring eyes.

I felt Alice's arms around me and heard her crying, "Fred! Are you all right? Fred!"

I tried to answer, but I couldn't.

When I heard her voice again, it was far away, and dwindling in the distance as darkness came and wrapped me up.

"Help!" she called. "Help! Please . . . somebody . . . help!"

THIRTEEN

When I woke up, I was tied down, spread-eagled, in a hospital bed, with my wrists and ankles strapped to its sides. There appeared to be a couple of dozen tubes stuck in me. They were connected with various bottles hanging from a frame around the bed.

"Well," I said, looking around. "This sure ain't heaven."

My voice echoed in the empty room. "Hey!" I yelled, "Is anybody out there?"

I waited. No answer. I hollered again. "Where the hell is everybody?"

The door opened and a big fat nurse rushed in. "Please don't shout, Mr. Frederickson," she puffed. "If you need me, use the buzzer."

"What buzzer?"

"It's near your pillow."

I glanced over and saw it. "What the hell am I supposed to push it with, my nose? You got me hogtied hand and foot."

"That's for your own protection, sir. You were so restless in the night, Doctor was afraid you might tear out the stitches."

"Well, I ain't restless now, so how about turning me loose?"

"I'll get Doctor," she said. Before I could stop her, she'd hustled out, her big behind shaking like a gunny sack full of jelly.

Carefully, I twitched what muscles I could move. I didn't feel any actual pain, but my whole right shoulder was filled with a dull ache. I found out later that it was my own butcher knife Mary Lou had used on me. I always keep it razor-sharp, so that gave her the chance to carve me up that much deeper.

My neck, where it scraped against my chin, was raw. I needed a shave. So I'd been here two, three days.

Where was Alice?

The door opened and the nurse came in again, followed by a slim young man in a white coat.

"Our patient's finally awake, Doctor," she chirped.

"How about untying me, Doc?"

He nodded, and Tiny began unstrapping me.

"How long have I been here?"

"Three days."

"How come I was out so long?"

"Mr. Frederickson, you were very nearly out for keeps. Medically speaking, you died in the ambulance. Your heart stopped twice. You're a very lucky man."

"I'm seventy years old and this is my first time in the hospital. How do you call that lucky? If I'd been lucky, that big old nigger woman'd never have got near me with her knife. She died, didn't she?"

Doc wouldn't meet my eye. "Perhaps we'll talk later about that. Tell me, how do you feel? Do you have any pain?"

"Ache in my shoulder." I waited. He didn't say anything, so I did. "She died all right. I saw her eyes when she went down." He still didn't say anything. "Where's Alice?"

"Mr. Frederickson," said the doc, "I'm under instructions not to discuss the case with you at this time."

He bent over and sniffed at my bandages.

"How do I smell?"

He laughed. "There's no sign of infection, but you could use a bath. Nurse, see to that. I think our patient's well enough for one."

"Send Alice in here," I said. "Let *her* give me my bath."

The doc looked at his watch. "We couldn't permit that. There *is* a visitor outside, but——"

Tiny had been trying all this time to slide a bedpan under me. I said, "I'm well enough to bounce Tiny here on her backside if she keeps poking around with that bedpan. So I reckon I can see a visitor."

Tiny went all red. "Really, Doctor."

The doc laughed again. "Help Mr. Frederickson into the bathroom if he asks you, Nurse. I doubt if there's anything *we* could do to damage him. He seems to be made of old inner tubes and baling wire anyway."

"Not to mention the shoe leather in my liver," I said.

143

"I'll send in your visitor," said doc, as he went out.

"Just help me sit up," I told Tiny. "And don't let my mouth scare you none. I like big women. If I didn't already have me one, you'd be next on my list, fat woman."

She fluffed my pillows. "Doctor's right, Mr. Frederickson. You're a very fortunate man."

"Tell you what, Tiny, you lock that door and crawl in here with me. What Alice don't know won't hurt her."

Tiny giggled. There came a knock at the door. Tiny started for it, saying over her shoulder, "Now, you be a good boy and ring for me if you have to go potty."

I growled and tried to throw a pillow at her, but the slightest movement made my shoulder hurt like hell. I winced, and cursed a little.

"Go right in," I heard Tiny say. "But don't tire him too much."

"I won't," said a man's voice.

I looked up.

By God, it was young Mr. Shaw, the assistant district attorney.

"Hey!" I said. "What the hell are *you* doing here?"

"I've been assigned to your case. How do you feel, Fred?"

"Like a sirloin steak, all carved up. How about Mary Lou? Did she die?"

"Yes," he said. "She died."

"What about the other one? The man? Did you catch him?"

144

"No. There *was* another one, then?"

"Sure there was. Didn't Alice tell you?"

He started to answer, then looked away.

"Hey, Mr. Shaw, where's Alice anyway?"

He hesitated. "Mr. Frederickson, I must advise you of your right to remain silent. If you give up the right to remain silent, anything you say can and will be used against you. You have the right to consult an attorney and have him present during questioning. If you cannot afford an attorney, one will be provided for you. Do you understand these rights?"

"Hot diggety damn!" I said. "I must have done something real bad. All of a sudden I got *rights!*"

"Do you want an attorney, Mr. Frederickson?"

"What do you think I should do, Mr. Shaw?"

He seemed embarrassed. "Off the record, I feel partly to blame for all this."

"All what?"

"Mary Lou. You don't really feel justice was done, do you?"

"Hell, no. If you near got choked to death by that big nigger woman and she stole all your money and used it to pay a slick lawyer and, by God, got *off,* would you think justice had been done?"

"Perhaps if the trial had turned out differently. Perhaps if I had explained things to you more carefully——"

"Hell, I know what happened. Good old Sid Michaelson was just too fast for you. He pulled all them postponements, and then when we lost Bernie as a witness, he lowered the boom."

145

"There's more to it than that. You see, Fred, there's no such thing as perfect justice. At best, it's a series of compromises, give and take."

"That's sure the truth. Except it seems like it's always us that's doing the giving and the Mary Lous that's doing the taking."

"The courts do their best. But with all the emphasis on individual rights today, particularly when the defendant is a member of the minority community, well, it's hard to throw the book at anyone anymore. In a minor infraction such as your assault, it's only sensible for the judge to avoid a long, drawn-out trial that would probably be a waste of time and, worse, further increase local tension."

"Mr. Shaw, I guess you can understand what you're getting at, but I sure in hell can't. You either got law for everyone, or you don't. Color don't enter into it."

He got impatient. "I was only trying to explain how, under the circumstances, the judge's decision was probably the correct one."

"Mr. Shaw, is there the slightest doubt in your mind that Mary Lou squoze my windpipe and stole all my money?"

"That's not the point here."

"Yes or no?"

"Well . . . I thought she was guilty, yes."

"How about your buddy, Sid?"

"Whatever he thought, it was his duty to provide the best defense he could——"

"That ain't what I asked you. Did old Sid think Mary Lou was guilty?"

"He *knew* she was. She admitted it to him. But——"

"How about the judge? Did *he* think she done it?"

"He may have suspected her guilt, but the judge can only be ruled by the evidence——"

"We never got a chance to *show* no evidence. But the judge, he's a man with a mind of his own just like the rest of us. Did he believe in his own mind that Mary Lou done it?"

"I suppose he did. After all, this wasn't the first time she had been before him on similar charges. But——"

"But what? There you was, the three of you, representing three sides of The Law, *knowing* she was guilty as sin, yet you all got your heads together and let her off. And then you act like you don't understand me when I say the kind of law you practice ain't no law at all. Well, I ain't no judge or lawyer neither, but I know enough to see you folks are barking up the wrong tree. You just can't let people run loose. There ain't no such thing as a *little* crime. You let somebody get away with busting windows and robbing cars and mugging old men in the elevator today, and by God, the fault sits square on you tomorrow when they graduate to killing folks. Just like Mary Lou tried to kill me, and she would have, too, if it hadn't been for Alice. If——"

I stopped. When I mentioned her name, he had looked away.

"Mr. Shaw, where *is* Alice?"

"Fred, you really ought to get a lawyer——"

"I said, where's Alice?"

"She's . . . ah . . . in the Women's House of Detention."

"The pokey? What the hell for?"

"This is most irregular. You really should have an attorney present."

"Screw that. How about giving me an answer?"

He put on a thin little pair of glasses and squinted at me through them. "Well, after all, she *did* kill a woman."

"Did no such thing. *I* shot Mary Lou, while she was carving up my gizzard."

Mr. Shaw shook his head. "Alice admitted the shooting, and nitrate tests of her hands confirmed that she'd fired a gun. She told us about the second person, the man, but under the circumstances——"

"Weren't no circumstances. You just didn't feel like believing her. All right, what if Alice *did* shoot Mary Lou? It was self-defense, wasn't it?"

"That's not easy to answer. The law requires that self-defense be undertaken only as a last resort. If it were possible to evade the attack, to run, to escape by any means, then the law does not recognize the presumption of self-defense——"

"Run! Get away! Hell, man, Mary Lou had me *down*! She was slicing me up like a Christmas turkey. How the hell was I going to run?" I glared up at him. "Does *Alice* have a lawyer?"

"Ah . . . well, no."

"Why not?"

"She was upset by what she had done. She refused legal assistance. She seemed to feel that she *should* be punished."

"And you, you rat bastard, you're doing all you can to see she gets her wish!"

"No, sir! At the proper time, she'll be provided with counsel, whether or not she requests it. Personally, I doubt that she'll even be charged with the homicide, because she *was* preventing the commission of a felony."

"In other words, she kept Mary Lou from killing me."

"Yes."

"Then why's she locked up?"

"Violation of Section Four, Paragraph Nine, of the New York State Weapons Act. Carrying a concealed weapon, to wit, one unlicensed thirty-two caliber automatic pistol——"

I stared at him. "Are you trying to say it's all right Alice shot Mary Lou to save my life, but that you got her locked up for *carrying* the gun she did it with?"

"The weapon was unlicensed, and Miss Gordon had no pistol permit. We had no choice."

"Of all the chickenshit——"

Stubbornly, Mr. Shaw said, "She should have gotten a permit."

"And how long would that have taken her?"

He looked out the window. "Well, lately, Albany's been discouraging their issuance. But six to eight weeks——"

"So if she'd gotten it at all, it would have been three or four weeks from now before she could have packed that gun without getting in trouble. Only I'd have been pushing up daisies all that time."

He spread his hands. "The law's the law, Fred."

"Is that a fact? How come The Law's the law for Alice and me, and it's only a big laugh for Mary Lou?"

"The courts are overcrowded, we do the best we can. . . ."

"Well, that ain't good enough, Mr. Shaw. It ain't good enough by a long shot. What about me? Am I under arrest, too?"

"Well——"

"Yes or no?"

"At the moment, no."

I reached over and pressed Tiny's buzzer. "In that case, Mr. Shaw, why don't you trot your flat ass out of here and get back to enforcing the laws against honest folks?"

"I'm not through questioning——"

"Unless you arrest me, you are."

The door opened and Tiny peeked in. I put on a croaking, dying old man's voice. "Nurse . . . I feel terrible porely and . . . this feller . . . won't leave. . . ."

She charged into the room, eyes blazing. "Out!"

Shaw protested, "But I'm with the district attorney's office. I——"

"*Out!*"

He went out mad, but he went.

I said, "Tiny, I love you."

She fluffed my pillow. "You should have buzzed for me sooner."

I sat up. "Bring me a telephone."

"But you need rest, you——"

"*Move,* fat woman!"

She hurried for the door. I yelled after her. "Tiny?"

"Yes, sir?"

"While you're out there, look up the phone number of a lawyer named Sid Michaelson."

FOURTEEN

"Disgraceful!" bellowed Sid Michaelson. "Shameful! I'll see that they pay for this flagrant——"

"What did you find out?" I asked.

After an hour of me yelling and threatening, the hospital had finally provided my room with two easy chairs. Sid Michaelson sat in one of them now, except when he was jumping up and waving his arms, and I was in the other.

"Completely unethical!" he stormed. "Abuse of the judicial process!"

"Sid, there ain't no jury here. Talk straight."

He simmered down. "They're holding her, all right. One phone call confirmed that. But they shouldn't be. If they'd arraigned her on the gun control charge, she'd be walking around free right now on her own recognizance. Or at most, a five-hundred-dollar bail."

"Then why ain't she out on bail?"

Sid lit up a fierce black cigar and puffed angry balls of smoke at me.

Alice and Me

"According to a friend of mine down at Center Street, she just didn't seem to care. Naturally, she's very depressed over the shooting. That's a normal reaction. According to my friend, she didn't care one way or the other whether or not they gave her her rights. So the D.A. didn't bother to push for an arraignment. He was obviously waiting to hear what you had to say, hoping you'd nail the lid a little tighter on her. As for Alice, once she knew that you were going to be all right, she apparently lost all interest in what happened to her personally."

"Get her out of there," I said.

Sid looked at his watch. "It's late in the day," he said. "I may not be able to swing it until tomorrow."

"No," I said. "You got to swing it today. Right now. She can't stay in there another night. Don't you see? It's all my fault. I don't care what it costs, just bust her out of there."

He cleared his throat. "About the matter of funds——"

"Don't you fret none about that. I got me four or five thousand bucks in cash stashed in the apartment. It's in a coffee can, sunk in the back of the toilet tank. Spend every goddamned nickel if you have to, but get that poor girl out of there!"

"I'll see what I can do," he said, starting for the door. "And, Fred——"

"Are you still here?"

"Don't worry about the money. It won't cost very much, and I don't think I'll even bill you. This one's on me, for getting Mary Lou off in the first place."

154

He went.

So. Just goes to show how wrong you can be when you jump to snap decisions. I felt real sorry now for saying those mean things in court about old Sid. You can't tell at all what a man's like by listening to what he says in public. It's behind the closed doors that the true person comes out, where nobody can see or take pictures.

Well, just like he said, Sid got Alice out. But something was bad wrong. He practically had to drag her up to the hospital. She didn't want to come anywhere's near me.

"Why the hell not?" I asked him.

"She's ashamed," Sid told me. Alice was waiting outside in the nurse's office, and Tiny had strict instructions not to let her skedaddle.

"Ashamed? What the hell for? Sid, I'm *proud* of her! She saved my goddamned life, didn't she? You should have been there! 'Don't you take another step toward him,' says Alice, and Mary Lou laughs and says, 'Tell that old man *good*bye,' and starts slicing at me with that pig-sticker, and Alice, cool as a cucumber, she cuts loose with that little thirty-two and ventilates Mary Lou like a Swiss cheese, just like I taught her."

Nervously, Sid said, "I wouldn't repeat that, Fred. About how you taught her."

"Why not? It's the truth. It was me taught Alice to shoot that gun."

"It's open to misunderstanding. It taints the presumption of self-defense with a definite suspicion of premeditation."

"If you say so. Mister, you keep hanging around and I'm going to have to hire me a translator."

"Fred," he said quietly, "be extremely careful when you talk to Alice. She's very disturbed."

"Do you think I'd hurt her? Sid, I love that gal, in my own silly way. I'd cut my hand off for her."

"I know you would," he said. "But maybe that's not what she wants." He got up. "I'll send her in."

While I waited there for her, patting down my robe and smoothing my hair, I couldn't help but feel a little helpless. They'd unplugged all the tubes, but I still couldn't get up and run down the road. My knees was too shaky for that. And my stomach was too, wondering what had happened to Alice. Hell's bells, all she did was shoot someone who deserved shooting. I never had any trouble doing that, why should she?

Alice came in. She wouldn't look at me. She kept staring at the floor.

"Hello, Fred. They say you're getting better."

My God, I saw what Sid had tried to tell me! She was all gone, just an empty husk that used to be my girl. Her hair was limp and faded, and her face looked puffy and doughy, like an unfinished gingerbread cookie. If I'd passed her on the street, a complete stranger, my first thought would have been, that's a sick woman.

"Yes, ma'am," I said, trying to make my voice cheery, "I'm up and around, thanks to you. You know you saved my life, don't you?"

"That's what they told me. I . . . have trouble re-membering."

I pulled her down in the chair beside me. "Alice, what's the matter?"

She kept staring at her fingers. They were dirty, and the nails were rimmed with black.

"There's nothing the matter," she said.

"Yes there is, Alice, and it breaks my heart to see you so tore up."

She didn't say nothing. Her face was blank. She was a stranger. And, while I tried to put it out of my mind, I couldn't help but notice that I could *smell* her. It was the dank, dead odor of old perspiration and fear.

I tried again. "If you're still fretting about Mary Lou, you shouldn't. That woman was death and destruction, just looking for a place to light. Somebody had to stop her. She was out to *get* us. I'm only sorry it had to happen to you instead of me. I didn't figure things would come out this way, believe me. All I had in mind was teaching you to protect yourself. I never thought in a million years that it'd end up with you protecting *me*."

Her voice was dull. She didn't seem the least bit interested in what she was saying. "Don't feel guilty about it, Fred. I don't. Not anymore."

"But I know it was an awful thing for you——"

She laughed. It sent a chill down my back. She sounded just like Mary Lou.

"Awful? That's all you know, old man." She leaned forward, and her eyes were bright. "I wish I could do it over again. I wish I could shoot *every fucking one of them*!"

157

I dragged myself out of the armchair and started over to her. She jumped up and grabbed hold of me and lowered me back into the chair.

"You crazy old man, what are you trying to do, kill yourself?"

Panting, I said, "Alice, what did they *do* to you in that jailhouse?"

She sank down to the floor and rested her head against my knee. "Oh, Fred," she said. "Don't talk. Don't ask questions. Not now." There was a long pause, then, "You should have gone to Wyoming. You don't belong here. *People* don't belong here."

I stroked her hair. "Poor Alice. I ain't brought nothing but misery to you. And that ain't what I meant to do, I swear it, girl."

"I know," she whispered. "It's all right. Don't blame yourself. Things happen. Things happen. . . ."

She pressed her face against my leg. She was crying.

"Are you sure you don't want to talk about it, Alice? It helps sometimes."

She muffled her voice against my knee. "No. It wouldn't help."

"Then you rest easy, Alice. I ain't going to press you."

"Thank you, Fred," she said in a far-off voice.

We sat there until it was good and dark outside. Tiny came in to turn on the lights, and I shook my head at her and she tiptoed out without making a sound.

Neither of us said another word. Twice, I felt her tears hot on my hand, but then they stopped, and there

was just the ragged sound of her breathing and trying
not to cry.

A long time later, Tiny tapped at the door and came
in.

"I'm sorry," she said. "But it's past nine, and Mr.
Frederickson just *has* to be in bed when the resident
makes his rounds."

Alice got up. "All right."

Tiny hesitated. "There's an empty room next door,
miss, if you'd like to stay. Nobody would have to
know."

"It doesn't matter," Alice said. "Thank you, but I'd
better go home."

"Are you sure, baby?" I asked.

"It doesn't matter," she repeated.

"Sid checked everything with Bernie," I said. "The
place is all cleaned up and locked. Bernie's got the key.
He put a police lock on this time. You don't have to
worry none."

"I won't," she said. "There's nothing left to worry
about."

She kissed me on the cheek.

"I'll probably come back in the morning," she said,
and left.

Tiny looked after her. "That poor girl," she said.
"She's so unhappy."

I didn't answer. If I'd tried to say a word, I would
have busted out crying.

It was a bad night. I tried to sleep, but all I could see
on the insides of my eyeballs was Alice, sitting there on

the floor, crying against my knee and staring at her hands like an old woman.

I have always been slow to anger, and I always fought it. Because if I ever get steamed up, the pressure stays there for a long time. And the only thing that'll let it off is for me to get rid of whoever put the pressure on to begin with. And that pressure was sure there now, rattling the safety valve.

But Alice had already removed Mary Lou, hadn't she? So why was I all lathered up?

Who else was bothering me?

How about *everybody*?

They'd been pushing me around ever since I hit town. Those punks in the park, the bank guard, Mary Lou—no matter which way I looked, somebody always had his foot out to trip me up.

I wished I had a drink. I didn't like lying there in the dark, listening to my heart pound.

The door slid open. A tall shadow of a figure came toward me.

"Who's that?" I asked.

"Me," said Alice's voice. "I came back. Fred, I'm afraid to be alone."

"You ain't the only one, big woman," I said. "Get in here with me."

"I can't! You're hurt."

"I just want you and me to snuggle up. I'm lonesome."

Her clothing rustled to the floor, and the bed sagged as she lowered herself onto it. I pulled her close. She was warm, but her arms trembled around my back.

"I'm glad you came back," I said.

"Fred . . ." she began.

"What is it, hon?"

"You won't love me anymore."

"I'll always love you," I said. "But remember what I said, I ain't the permanent kind."

"Are you still afraid I'll try to tie you down?" her voice was almost like the old Alice.

"Nope. You can't get a rope on me unless I put out my wrists, and I don't aim to."

"Oh, Fred," she said, stroking my shoulder.

"Come on, hon," I said. "Let it out."

"Are you sure you want to hear?"

"No, to be honest, I wish I didn't have to. But I do. So go ahead. It's just you and me, it's all right."

"They were laying for me. They run the jails, and I killed one of them, and they were waiting."

"Who?"

"You know." Her voice faltered. "The niggers."

"Alice! You never used that word before."

"I never *had* to before. Those weren't blacks or colored or Negroes. They were *niggers,* and I hate every fucking one of them!"

"What did they do?"

"Little things at first. They split up into two sides. One side was overly polite, big smiles, all teeth and swollen lips. 'We doan want no trouble,' they told me. 'We *protecting* you against the others.' Of course, there was a small price for the protection. They took my cigarettes, my personal things that the matron had let me keep. It wasn't much. Lipstick, my comb. But precious,

161

when that's all you have left in the world. I gave them whatever they wanted, though. Oh, Fred, I was so *afraid*. It didn't take any genius to see that they *ran* the jail. The guards were on the outside, to keep us in. And that's all they worried about. *In*side, the strongest group controlled everything. Do you know what they call newcomers like me? Fresh fish. None of the fresh fish have it easy, but I had it harder than most, because of Mary Lou."

She pulled me closer. "Some of the old-timers, prostitutes, mostly, tried to help me. But they couldn't. One of them, a horrid old woman who must have been sixty, told me that the lesbian gangs used to run things. They could, because they'd stick together, while the regular inmates wouldn't. Instead of protecting each other, they'd let themselves be victimized one at a time, because each of them hoped that'd she'd be the one who wasn't molested. It's the same now, except this time it's the niggers making up most of the power structure. You can't fight just one black woman. They gang up on you. Every one within throwing distance will hit you with something. They get their kicks out of it. Outside, they're a minority. My God, Fred, I used to go on marches to try and get them more rights! Inside, they've got the power, and they get their revenge, and baby, do they have *fun!*"

"What else happened?" I said, trying to keep my voice from shaking.

"Well, they 'protected' me. All day and all night, Mary Ann. I didn't get a wink of sleep. They kept me up, describing the little delights the 'others' had in

store for me. After a while, I fell into a complying daze.
I'd move where they told me, sit where they told me,
eat what they told me. I went to the bathroom when
they told me. Then, just before dawn of the third
morning, when I'd completely stopped thinking and was
only *reacting*, like a beaten animal, they suddenly
turned on me. Cowards! They outnumbered me ten to
one, but still they waited to be sure I had nothing left
before taking the chance. They stuffed my mouth with
dirty rags, and two of them sat on my arms and chest to
hold me down, and then, one by one, they came to
me. . . ."

She stopped, crying. I hugged her close.

"Don't say no more, Alice."

"Fred," she whispered, "Why did you let them do it?
Why didn't you *kill* them?"

"Shhhh . . . shhhh. . . ."

She shuddered in my arms. My heart pounded and
my mind raced, but I tried to hold still.

"Why?" she asked.

I couldn't answer her.

But, by God, I would when I got out of this hospital!
If it wasn't for Alice, I probably would have just
turned around and walked off. My hide's too tough to
damage it permanently. But when they turned loose on
my woman, they made this my personal business. I
don't let nobody come after me and mine.

Next morning, when Tiny tiptoed in, she raised her
eyebrows at Alice sleeping there with me, but that good
old gal, she didn't say nothing. When she left, I shook
Alice, and she sat up.

"Fred!"

"It's me, honey."

"Have I been here all night?"

"Snug as a bug in a rug."

"I dreamed. . . ."

I kissed her. "It don't matter. Dreams don't count, Alice. But you better get up before that gang of interns shows up to practice medicine on my weary bones. How do you feel?"

She slipped into her clothes. "I don't know. Better. Like things really . . . hadn't happened."

"Good," I said. "Now, you go on home and let me worry about everything."

She left, and they shoved some oatmeal and stewed prunes at me, and then Sid showed up.

"Sid," I asked, "how do we get Alice off?"

"It's tough," he said unhappily. "She made a statement and signed it. She admitted she was carrying the gun."

"That poor girl was out of her head with grief," I said. "How would she know what she was saying?"

Sid pursed his lips and took out one of those evil black cigars. He bit the end off and lit up. "Shaw doesn't *really* want to prosecute her," he said slowly. "But he's stuck in the middle. He's got to go through the motions to keep those antigun nuts off his back. It isn't popular today to go around shooting people, even to save lives."

"That's a stuck record," I said. "There must be something we can do. What is it?"

"If only the mayor didn't spend two days a week

screaming against guns and the people who own them. . . ."

"I ain't interested in the mayor. What about Alice?"

"Her statement might be overthrown," he said. "That is, if it turned out there was a reasonable doubt that the weapon was actually in her possession. . . ."

Sid stopped and looked at me. I didn't need no road sign. I got his message. He couldn't come right and *tell* me what to say. But he'd hinted broad enough.

"Hell, that ain't no problem," I said. "I know for a fact that she wasn't carrying no gun. How could she, when that big black man, the one that got away, *he* was the one who had it?"

"How did it get into Alice's hands?" Sid asked gently.

"I saw him drop it when he run out the door and bumped into me. I guess Alice picked it up."

Sid knocked some ash off his cigar. "Could be. But the police found an extra-clip in her purse. What about that?"

"Is *that* what she picked up in the hall just before I opened the door? I saw her bend over and find something. It was pretty dark, but now that I think of it, that's what it must have been."

"Our mysterious burglar had a real case of the dropsies, didn't he?"

"Do you mean the judge won't believe us?"

"Of course not. Nobody in his right mind would accept that story."

I sat back. "So Alice is still in trouble."

Sid shook his head and exhaled a cloud of black smoke. "Not necessarily. You see, Fred, it doesn't matter if they believe us or not, so long as we can offer them a reasonable alternative to let them save face and preserve the appearance of due process." He fogged up the room some more. "Yes, it might just work. In fact, if we present our side of the story properly to the district attorney's office, the case might never come to trial at all."

"What about Alice's confession?"

"*Confession*? An unwitnessed statement taken in a back room under great emotional strain, without benefit of an attorney's advice? Ha! Don't make me laugh."

"You're a good man, Sid Michaelson. Keep it from going to trial. I don't care how you work it. We can't let that girl go through any more misery. If you have to pay off somebody, pay, but *do* it."

"I might have to get to one property clerk down at Center Street," he said. "If we're lucky, he could lose that extra clip."

"Sid, do anything. We can't let them hurt her anymore."

"They won't," he said. "You've got my word."

FIFTEEN

Sid's word was good. The charges against Alice were dropped.

She didn't seem to care. The world was something outside that she didn't pay no mind to. She just sat around the house and watched TV and drank beer. She started putting on weight.

Meanwhile, I was busy. There was things I had to do. You don't set out to accomplish what I had in mind without making some preparations. I went down and traded my Kansas driver's license for one from Albany, and I hired me a little machine shop and worked in it for a couple of evenings with a welding torch. When I was ready, I told Alice, "We're going back up to Roscoe."

She answered, "All right," in a voice that wasn't any more interested than if I'd said, "Let's have another beer."

This time we rented a car from Avis, on Broadway,

and headed up. I had it in mind to bring back some stuff that I didn't want no bus driver snooping through.

As we drove over the George Washington Bridge, Alice popped us each a beer.

I sipped. "Alice," I said, "I been doing a whole lot of thinking about everything that's happened, and I'd like to talk about it some."

"All right," she said.

"You ain't been having a good time lately, have you?"

"I don't know," she said. "I guess not."

"Well, I don't blame you. There's some things you don't forget easy. But you got to understand, hon, no matter where you go, there's bound to be *some* bad people. The reason there's more of them in the city is because there's more people there."

"What do I care?" she asked. "It happened. I don't care what the odds were."

"Good!" I said. "That's the spirit. Don't let the sons of bitches off. That's what's wrong, they always get off."

"But what can we do?"

"Well, the way I see it, we got us two choices. One, we can just take off. I got enough money, we can head out to Wyoming and build us an A-frame, and spend the winter hunting and sitting by the fireplace."

"I don't care," she said dully. "It really doesn't matter."

I had been afraid she'd say that. So it wouldn't do her any good at all to take her out west. The poison was infected too deep to come out by itself.

"Maybe there's another way," I said slowly.

"What?" But she wasn't really interested.

"Maybe we could go back to the city and *get* those bastards."

She stiffened. "What do you mean, *get* them?"

I turned up Route 17 past the Motel on the Mountain and while I drove, I told her.

While Alice was checking us into the Antrim Lodge, I went over to see the good old gal at the Bow and Arrow.

Sipping at a Utica Club, I asked, "You got a big walk-in reefer, don't you?"

"A refrigerator? Yes."

"I wonder if you'd do a little favor for me. Can you get hold of some empty milk cartons? Say a dozen?"

"That's easy," she said. "I've got that many out back right now."

"Good. Now take and fill them up with Jello and put them in that reefer until they firm up."

"Jello? Twelve *quarts* of Jello?"

"That's what I need. Can you help me?"

She shrugged. "Why not? Any particular flavor?"

I started to say, "It doesn't matter," then I stopped and said, "Make them cherry. Nice and red."

Alice came in. "We got our old room," she told me.

"How are you, dear?" asked the lady.

"Fine," said Alice, and her voice was almost perky, now that she had started cheering up again.

"What are you two up to?" asked the lady. "Are you planning a Jello orgy?"

Alice asked her what she was talking about, and the lady explained and Alice laughed. That made me feel good. It was the first time I'd seen her laugh since that night in the hallway.

"Fred hasn't mentioned any orgy to me," she said. "But if there's one lined up, I hope he picked a flavor I like."

"He wants cherry," said the lady.

"Yum," said Alice.

"I do believe both of you are crazy," said the woman. But she was smiling.

"Big woman," I told Alice, "I said it before, and I'll say it again——"

"I know," she said. "I've got a dirty mind. And don't you love it?"

I took a big swig of my beer and smiled. Things was getting back to normal.

They was normal that night in bed, too.

"Your *shoulder!*" Alice warned. "Be careful, Fred!"

But it didn't cause us no trouble at all.

After, in the dark, she put her head on my chest. Softly, she said, "Are you really going to do this? Just for me?"

"For *us,*" I said. "I got tired of being kicked around, too."

"But it's against the law."

"You already know what I think of The Law. What do they expect me to do, when they come after me and mine? Look to The Law? What good does that do? No, Alice, we're through with The Law. They don't care what happens to us as long as we don't make too much noise about it."

"If we do what you're planning," Alice whispered, "there'll be plenty of noise. They'll care plenty. They'll *have* to."

Next morning, I said, "You go over to the Bow and Arrow and get all that Jello. Have her pack it in a cardboard box with some ice to keep it firm. I'll pick you up there in maybe an hour."

"Be careful," she said.

"Don't worry. He won't have any idea what I'm up to."

I drove over to the gunsmith's garage-front store. He was out in front this time, stacking up boxes of ammo. When I came in, he gave me a worried look.

"I hope there hasn't been any trouble with——"

"No trouble," I said. "I just come in to buy me a rifle."

He was still uneasy. "You need a New York State driver's license or some other proof of residency," he said. "I'm not allowed to sell long guns to out-of-staters——"

"Got it right here," I said, putting my brand new operator's license up on the counter.

He relaxed. "Good. I mean, we wouldn't want to break the law, would we, Mr. Frederickson?"

"Only if it was profitable," I said, staring at him. He got uneasy again. Then I gave him a short laugh. "Just kidding around. Now, about that rifle?"

"What did you have in mind?"

"Thought I'd ask *you* about that. I want something that will reach out two, three hundred yards, and get *out* there, too. Real fast."

"Do you plan to use it for hunting or for target shooting?"

"To be safe, let's say a little of both."

He considered the rack of guns behind the counter. "Well, there's always the thirty-ought-six. Are you planning to hand-load your ammo?"

"I don't think so. Probably won't have time."

"Even so, the ought-six'll go out at twenty-six hundred feet a second firing the hundred and eighty grain soft point. That'll bring down any game you'll find on the North American continent, if you hit it right."

"I've shot the ought-six," I said. "Had one up in Alaska. It's a good gun. Could be. Let's try one. What else do you have?"

"Well, there's the two-seventy. It's considerably faster than the ought-six. Your factory loads will give you muzzle velocities up to thirty-one hundred feet per second. And the trajectory is flatter than the ought-six, of course. The two-seventy drops only six inches at three hundred yards."

"Got to try that one, too," I said. "What I had in mind was to take out three or four guns and test fire them before I make up my mind which one to buy. Is that okay with you?"

"Sure. If you want to do some shooting without anyone bothering you, take the old mountain road, over toward the reservoir. Go about six miles and you'll come across a flat field to the left with a hill behind it. That's a perfect two-hundred-yard range."

"Fine. I'll shoot the ought-six and the two-seventy. What else do you have?"

"Well, there's this little twenty-two two-fifty. It's a twenty-two slug on top of a hell of a lot of powder, almost as much as you get in an ought-six case. If the wind's not bad and you don't have to shoot through brush, it'll get right out there. It leaves the muzzle at almost four thousand feet a second. Only trouble is, it's moving so fast that it'll blow up if it hits even a leaf."

I whistled. "That's some fast. Blowing up like that ain't so bad, is it? I mean, it wouldn't ricochet around much, would it?"

"Not a chance. When it hits, it explodes."

"That's a lot safer for the innocent bystanders," I said.

"What?"

"No matter. Let me try that one, too."

All three guns had telescopic sights. I took four rounds of ammo for each of them and a big sandbag to use as a rifle rest. I told the gunsmith I'd be back in a couple of hours, packed the guns in the trunk, and drove over to pick up Alice.

She put the Jello in the back seat and got in.

Nodding toward the Bow and Arrow, she said, "She thinks we're crazy, all that Jello."

"Let her keep thinking it. What she doesn't know won't hurt us."

"How could she know anything? *I* don't even know, Fred. What's all the Jello for?"

"We're going to have us a Jello orgy," I said. I started up the car. Alice fell back against the seat, laughing. It was a good sound to hear.

I found the target field without any trouble and told her, "Take that box of Jello cartons up there and line them up in a row against that fence. Put them around a foot apart."

She stared. "Why?"

"You just do like I say. You'll see."

She shook her head and started off up the hill. I took out the three rifles. Before I loaded them, I put the sandbag down on a little knoll, sprawled myself out in the rifleman's prone position, and snugged the thirty-ought-six down on the sandbag. When I squinted through the sight, it was as steady as a rock. I could almost count Alice's eyelashes.

I got up again and loaded the rifles. The thirty-ought-six and the two-seventy both had internal magazines. I slid four cartridges into each of them. The twenty-two two-fifty had a clip, and I clicked four rounds into it and rammed it home in the gun's belly.

Alice came back. "What do we do now?"

"Now you just watch," I said, stretching out behind the sandbag with the thirty-ought-six.

I estimated that the milk cartons of Jello were just about as far away as the gunsmith had said, two hundred yards, so I put the cross hairs right on the carton's top third, just where a little man's chest would be, and squeezed off a round. The rifle went "KA-BLAM!" and snugged up against my shoulder with that good old feeling I'd almost forgotten.

Alice shaded her eyes, looking at the milk carton. "It didn't move. You must have missed."

"Quiet, big woman," I said. I squoze off the other three rounds, aiming in turn at the next three cartons.

Then I switched to the two-seventy. It didn't have

quite as much recoil as the ought-six, but the muzzle report still had a loud voice, echoing against the hills.

Finally, I drew down on the last four cartons with the little twenty-two two-fifty. It didn't kick at all, and while its "SPLAT!" came back from the hills with authority, it didn't make anywhere near so much noise as the other two.

I opened the bolts on all three rifles, checked the chambers, and put them back in the car trunk and locked it.

"Let's see how we did," I said.

Alice followed me up the field. When we got close to the cartons, she let out a little cry.

"You *did* hit them!"

"Sure I did. I'd be ashamed to miss at this distance."

Besides, I'd made sure from the gunsmith that all three guns were zeroed in at two hundred yards and were more or less shooting straight. Of course, I'd have to fine-tune whichever one I bought to fit it to my own eye. But as we got close, I could see that I'd hit all twelve of the cartons within an inch or so of where I'd been holding the sights, and that was damned good shooting for guns right off the rack. I decided that the gunsmith probably knew his business.

Alice was examining the cartons. "There's just a little hole going in," she said, "but the whole back is blown away."

"That's what the Jello was for," I told her. "It's the closest thing you can get to human flesh for making a bullet expand on impact."

The four cartons I'd hit with the thirty-ought-six

were tore up pretty good, and so were the ones I'd hit with the two-seventy. But the ones that amazed me were the four I had shot with the twenty-two two-fifty.

The little .22 slug had made only a tiny hole punching through the waxed cardboard, and it hadn't even come *out* at all. Instead, the bullet had exploded right in the middle of the Jello, distorting and distending the carton's sides, and, most surprising, actually liquefying the Jello.

I picked up one of the cartons and, slowly, poured out the thick, red liquid.

"If that was a man's brains," I said, "he'd be in real trouble."

Alice didn't answer, but there was a dull glare in her eyes.

I bought the little twenty-two two-fifty for $99.50, including a 4X Weaver scope and an extra clip.

"I thought you might pick that one," said the gunsmith. "It ain't legal in this state, but you could bring down a deer easy with that bullet."

"That's not what I had in mind," I said, paying him.

I went over to the hardware store and got some tools and the other stuff I needed, and stopped at the Esso station for a road map.

While Alice and me had a beer at the Bow and Arrow, I marked out a route for her on the map.

"I want you to take the back roads," I said. "Hit Livingston Manor, and Sloe, and Downsville, and all those other little towns. Park your car a couple of blocks away so they don't see the license plates, and hit every sporting-goods and hardware store you can find. Buy two boxes of twenty-two two-fifty hollowpoints in each one. No more. They won't question you for that. If they do ask for ID, show them this."

I gave her a driver's license made out to Cora West of Morris, New York. Bernie had provided it for another of my fifty-dollar bills when I asked him for a woman's ID that couldn't be traced.

Alice didn't comment either. She nodded and put the license in her purse. I gave her two hundred dollars, kissed her on the mouth, and said, "Drive careful. You don't want to get picked up."

"I'll be careful," she said.

I went out to the car with her and took out the gear I'd bought at the hardware store. She drove off slowly without looking back.

I stopped at the liquor store and bought a quart of Jack Daniels. Then I went up to our room and locked the door.

First, I used a hacksaw to cut nine inches off the rifle barrel. It was good steel, and hard work to cut through, and took the best part of an hour. I wore out three hacksaw blades. When I got finished, I was sweating and my hands were all cramped, so I took a breather and a good slug of Jack. Then I measured the inside of the aluminum Halliburton case I'd brought up from the city. Its top and bottom were both filled with foam rubber, and there was a little Xacto knife for cutting recesses in it.

It would take an object just twenty-nine inches long.

I took a pipe cutter and threaded the front of the cut-off rifle barrel. It wasn't neat, but it would do.

I took a regular saw, then, and cut off the wooden stock, just behind the trigger assembly. I used sandpaper to smooth down the raw wood and screwed two round clips to it.

In my suitcase was the wire Luger stock I'd bought at an antique gun shop down in the city. The two bare ends clicked perfectly into the clips, and I had a skeleton stock that nestled up against my shoulder just as good as the original wooden one.

The silencer probably wasn't necessary, because the twenty-two two-fifty was quieter than I'd figured on, and what's more, I didn't intend to fire more than one shot at a time. No one, no matter how alert, can pinpoint the location of a single unexpected rifle shot. Most people don't even recognize it as one. But I'd spent eleven hours in that rented machine shop, welding tiny baffles inside a chunk of two-inch pipe, and since I already had it, I might as well use the thing. The silencer would only add around six ounces to the whole package, and anyway it would mask muzzle blast at night.

The threads mated perfectly. I screwed the silencer onto the cut-off barrel, hoisted the completed weapon to my shoulder, and squoze off a dry run.

The hammer went *click*! in the silent bedroom.

The rifle was a little front-heavy, but nothing that would bother me.

I slid a clip into it, detached the skeleton stock, and

laid the rifle down on the rubber inside the Halliburton case. I traced its outline with a Bic Banana magic marker, took the Xacto knife and cut out a recess, and the sawed-off rifle snugged down inside the case like it had been born there.

To finish up, I cut out holes in the foam rubber for the skeleton stock, the extra clip, and two boxes of ammo.

I packed it all inside, closed the case, picked it up, and looked at myself in the full-length door mirror.

"Hot diggity damn," I said. "I look just like a traveling salesman."

SIXTEEN

The gun had shot all right when I'd tried it out, but shortening the barrel and putting the silencer on would have an effect. I'd have to zero it all over.

Alice got back all right with the ammunition. Like I'd told her, she'd bought it two boxes at a time, all over the Catskills. Altogether, she got eleven hundred rounds. That figured to be more than enough, so we wouldn't have to buy anymore. This was extra protection for us, because I had a hunch that once we got started, the word would go out fast to investigate anybody buying twenty-two two-fifty shells.

We went back up on the hill where I'd shot the Jello cartons. This time I took along a big cardboard box and some nine-inch paper plates that I'd marked in the middle with an inch-square rectangle.

Alice put the box up near the fence, and I paced off the distance to be sure it was within spitting range of two hundred yards. I came out with two hundred and five, which was close enough.

I slipped a round in the chamber, rested the gun on the sandbag, centered the paper plate in the scope, and squoze off. Alice, who was sitting on the grass in front and about twenty yards to the left of the target, shouted, "Miss! You didn't even hit the cardboard box."

Like I figured, the gun was shooting way off now. But I could fix that.

I pulled the bolt out and put it aside, then snugged the rifle down on the sandbag rest.

Bore sighting isn't that hard, once you get a good steady rest. What you do is look right through the rifle barrel at the target, then match that view up with the sights. I got the barrel lined up with the paper plate. Then, without moving anything, I looked through the scope.

The cross hairs were high and to the right. I took off the adjustment caps and turned the little screws inside to move the cross hairs. Then I checked again, first looking through the barrel and then through the scope.

I'd adjusted a little too far to the left. I turned the windage screw two clicks back to the right. Elevation looked good.

I put the bolt back in and fired another round.

This time, Alice called, "On the plate. Dead center but a little high."

I took the elevation adjustment down a click, and fired three more rounds to get a group. Then I walked up to look at the target.

The slugs had bunched up in the center of the plate. They were all touching the black.

"That's good enough," I said. "If that plate was a man's head, he'd be mighty sick right now."

"It's so *quiet*," Alice said. "All I heard was a kind of *pffft* noise."

"We don't want to attract any more attention than we have to," I said. "Well, this thing's shooting straight. Now let's try it out."

"But you just did," she said.

"Not really," I said, walking back to the car. "It's one thing to shoot at paper. It's something else to shoot at flesh and blood. You ought to know that by now."

"Yes," she said. "I suppose I do."

It was late afternoon. We drove back toward Roscoe and parked just past the bridge over the little stream. I opened the glove compartment, got the new Buck hunting knife I'd bought, and stuck it in my hip pocket.

"Get that big plastic bag I put in the back seat," I told Alice. It was a heavy-duty thirty-gallon garbage bag. She did.

"What are you going to do?" she asked as we trudged up the hill, the silver Halliburton case banging against my leg.

"You'll see," I said. "And maybe you won't like it."

It was cool. My breath made little clouds of smoke in the still mountain air.

We got up to the place above the apple orchard and sat down on the same tree we'd been on before. I unpacked the rifle and assembled it.

"This is where we saw the deer," Alice said. "What are we doing here?"

"Waiting."

"Fred! You're not!"

"Hush up, woman," I said. "Don't tell me how to do my business."

"But *why*? You can't mean to kill those beautiful animals!"

"I got my reasons. Now be still. We don't want to spook them."

"I'll scream," she said. "I'll make a noise when they come out and scare them away."

"You do that little thing," I told her, "and the whole thing's off."

"But we're not mad at *them*," she protested.

"I know it, Alice," I said. "Now will you be still?"
She sulked, but she stayed quiet.

Just before the sun went down, the big old doe came out with her two fawns. I lifted the rifle and found her in the scope. She would have been an easy shot. Her shoulder filled the picture. Alice hissed in her breath. I put the rifle down.

"Don't worry," I said, low. "It ain't her I'm after."

The herd gathered slowly, and I scoped them all. I didn't see no horns. It was getting dark. We didn't have too much more time.

I pulled the rifle up and laid the cross hairs on one doe who had been keeping to herself over in one corner of the orchard. She was going gray, and looked almost mouse-colored.

"Fred," Alice whispered.

My finger, which had been squeezing, loosened on the trigger. I lifted my head and looked over the rifle barrel.

The big buck had come out into the field. His head was high as he sniffed the air.

"That's the one," I said.

I put the cross hairs right on his forehead and began closing my hand. The trigger squeeze on the twenty-two two-fifty was so easy you never knew when she was going to touch off.

Just as she did, and the metal stock bucked lightly against my shoulder, and the silencer made a *pffft!* cough, the buck turned his head. I heard the slap of the bullet, and he fell like an invisible scythe had cut all four legs out from under him.

The rest of the herd scattered.

I ejected the empty and got up. I could hear Alice crying.

"Come on, big woman," I said. "Let's go down there. And bring that plastic bag."

She stumbled after me. "Oh, Fred," she choked. "He was so beautiful."

"He ain't nothing but meat now," I told her.

When we got there, Alice looked down at the buck and turned her head and began throwing up. He wasn't pretty, I'll admit. The slug had exploded and taken off the whole side of his head. One eye was bulging out like a grape on a stalk.

"It ain't like the movies, is it, girl?" I said. "There, when a feller gets shot, he may limp a little, but he can still climb a tree and beat hell out of the bad guy. Well, that's not the way it happens. A bullet don't make a nice neat little wound and then go on its way. It blows up inside, and turns the flesh to jelly. Look at it, Alice.

185

I want you to see. That's one of the reasons I done this. You got to know what we're getting into."

She trembled, but she looked.

"Well?" I said. "Is this what you want to do? Do you want to put a man down like this and turn him into meat?"

Alice bent over slowly and put her trembling hand into the buck's thick, crimson blood.

"Yes," she whispered.

"You sure now, gal?"

"Yes."

"He can't get up again and prance away. Never again. So you got to be sure."

"Goddamnit, Fred, I *said* I'm sure!"

"Just so's you know," I said.

I gutted him out where he lay on the ground. It's harder that way, but I didn't have no rope to string him up with. Fascinated, Alice watched as I pulled out the lumpy, shining guts. The deer's blood steamed in the coolness of the evening.

"I never knew blood smoked," Alice said.

As I cut the dark brown liver free, I said, "It smokes, all right, when the air's cool like this. Hold open that sack."

She did, and I dropped the liver into it. Then I cut the heart away from the lungs and put it into the bag too.

"What are we going to do with those things?" Alice asked.

"We're going to eat them," I told her.

We were driving back from Roscoe on Route 17. It was almost midnight, and the resort traffic was thinning out. The Halliburton case sat innocently in the trunk with our suitcases and the bag of deer heart and liver. The radio was on, playing "The Beautiful Ohio Waltz."

"Why did you cut the antlers off and put them in a tree?" Alice asked.

"The birds'll eat them out," I said. "Up there, the field mice won't get into them. Maybe some hunter'll find them and take them home to nail up on his barn. You don't want to waste a good set of antlers."

"I was afraid," she said softly. "Then I put my hand in the blood, and it wasn't that bad after all. I guess I thought blood was something magic, that it would burn your skin or cry out. But it's just warm and red."

"That's the beginning," I said. "When I was only a kid, I sort of figured I was something special, that there wasn't any meat or guts inside *me*. But after you cut open a few animals, you start thinking differently, and that's when you learn that you ain't nothing special after all, that if a knife or a bullet gets you right, you'll stink up the place just the same as some gut-shot antelope.

"When do we start?" she asked.

"No big hurry," I said. "We want to work our way into it careful-like. No sense in going off half-cocked and getting caught before we even get moving. Because, Alice, you just *know* The Law ain't going to understand what we're doing, and they sure in hell ain't going to award us no medals."

"What law?" Alice said. "I haven't seen any law around here lately."

"That's the truth."

She leaned toward me, her eyes shining kind of strange. "I want to go with you the first time," she said.

"Now, don't go getting ideas, big woman. I ain't going to let you go up on those roofs with me, so don't get your hopes up."

In a voice that I'd only heard when we was in bed together, Alice said, "Then you've got to describe everything to me. I've got to *know!*"

"You'll know," I said. "I won't hold nothing back when it happens."

Touching my arm, she said, "Let it happen soon, Fred."

I didn't answer. The car bored its way through the darkness. The headlights pointed our way over the bridge and back to the apartment.

There wasn't any interesting mail. Another check from the Deep Balm people. I remembered I hadn't even gotten around to cashing the last one. Once you got enough money, any more seems kind of boring.

As soon as we was in the bedroom, Alice said, "Let me look at it again. I want to hold it."

"Alice," I said. "You got to try and keep yourself down. That rifle ain't nothing but a tool. In itself, it's nothing."

"I know. But please."

So I opened up the Halliburton case, and she run her hands over the dull metal of the barrel. Her fingers fluttered past the bolt and the trigger assembly, and the gleaming tube of the telescopic sight.

"It's beautiful . . . just like a big——"

I laughed.

Defensively, she said, "Well, that's what it *does* look like."

"That's what a lot of them newspaper writers say. Me, all I see is a rifle. This here is a Remington Model Six-seven-seven, caliber twenty-two dash two-fifty. It fires a fifty-three grain hollowpoint slug with a muzzle velocity of thirty-eight hundred and ten feet a second, and it'll blow up a man's head just like hitting a watermelon with an axe."

I took a silicone cloth and wiped down the metal where she'd touched it.

"No fingerprints?" she said.

"No rust. Ain't nothing'll rust a gun quicker than the skin oil on your fingers."

I closed the case and put it away in the closet.

We had us a couple of drinks, but it was like there was a stranger in the apartment with us. Alice kept glancing at the closet door.

"Why *wait*?" she asked.

"I told you, Alice, we don't want to jump into this thing."

Her voice was shrill. "You don't want to jump at all. You'll just put it off and put it off and *never* do it!"

"Don't lean on me, woman."

"Then *do* it!"

"I know what I'm up to."

Bitterly, she said, "So do I."

She went into the bathroom and closed the door.

I worked on my drink, but it had lost its taste.

I tapped on the bathroom door. She didn't answer. I pushed it open. She was sitting on the closed john seat, staring into the empty tub.

"All right," I said. "Come on. We might as well get it over. You can even watch, this time. You got it due you."

"Fred!"

"Remember, Alice, never again. You ever sharpen your tongue on me once more and that's all she wrote."

She covered my face with quick, nibbling kisses. "I won't, Fred. I'm sorry."

I didn't kiss her back, I was so mad. "Okay," I said, opening up the closet door. "Come on."

We both put on dark raincoats and gloves. I checked inside the Halliburton case to be sure everything was there.

"Ready?"

"Yes," said Alice.

We locked the door with the new police lock and caught a downtown bus. At Lincoln Center, we got off. I had already picked out a building to use. It had an elevator that went up to the penthouse floor, where there was a little alcove with two windows overlooking the fountain in front of the New York State Theater. Both penthouses were dark, so we wouldn't even have to go out on the roof, just raise one of the windows a few inches.

I took the pair of ten-power binoculars out of the little harness I'd fastened inside my raincoat and glassed the sidewalks and the Lincoln Center mall.

"What do you see?" Alice asked, anxiously.

"Just people. There ain't nothing much going on."

"Let me look."

She took the glasses, swept them over the street nine stories below. Then she looked over on the other side. She leaned forward.

"There!" she cried. "Down near the subway entrance, that big man who's just standing around."

I put the glasses on him. He was a big fat white man. He had both hands jammed down in his pockets. He wasn't doing anything special. But Alice was right. He just didn't look natural.

"Maybe he's only tired," I said. "Or sick."

"I think he's up to something," she said. "Keep watching him."

"I will. Open up that case."

I heard the latches click.

"Now, keep the lid down so if somebody comes up the elevator, they won't see the gun."

"It's done."

I didn't take my eyes off the fat man. He shifted from one foot to the other, looked around, spat on the sidewalk.

Three women came out of a restaurant and started for the subway. The fat man seemed to come alert at the sight of them. He made a big show of peering across the street, like he'd spotted an old friend. Then, without watching where he was going, he started across and busted right into the little group of women. Handbags and hats fell like rain.

The fat man could be seen to be apologizing profusely as he helped the women pick up their belongings. They thanked him and went off on their way.

"Did he?" Alice asked.

"He did," I said. He had been slick, but through the ten-power glasses, I'd seen his hand dip into one of the purses, remove the fat wallet, and drop it in his overcoat pocket, all in one smooth, unsuspicious movement. "Robbed a wallet."

I heard the Halliburton case lid bang against the wall as she opened it. Without taking my eyes off the fat man, I felt for the rifle, slipped the skeleton stock into the holders. I'd put the field glasses down to have both hands free, and Alice grabbed them.

"Hurry!" she said. "He'll get away."

"No he won't," I said. I operated the bolt and jacked a shell into the chamber. "He's real cool. He ain't in no hurry."

I pushed the window up and poked the rifle out. I had to fish around with the scope to find him, slouching across Broadway with both hands jammed down in his pockets again.

"He's going to flag a cab," Alice warned.

"Not in this world, he ain't," I said. I lined the cross hairs up just behind his ear.

With the scope settled into place, I took a deep breath, let it out, and by squeezing the trigger ever so gently, blew the fat man's brains all over a passing truck.

"Well," I said, "That's number one."

SEVENTEEN

Oh, there was a commotion, all right.

Watching through the glasses, Alice described it to me as I packed the rifle back up in the case.

"He's still down," she said. "He hasn't even twitched. When you hit him, his legs went out from under him like someone'd yanked them with a rope. There are a lot of people gathering around. They must think he's had some kind of fit."

They wouldn't have heard the shot, of course. Even in the enclosed alcove, it hadn't made much more than a sort of metallic *spang*! sound.

"They've seen the blood now," Alice said, her voice vibrating with excitement. "They're looking around."

I closed the case. "Let's go."

She handed me the binoculars. I put them inside my coat and shut the window.

The elevator was still waiting where we'd left it, on the top floor.

Alice and Me

As we descended, Alice gripped my arm. "We did it."
"Mind what you say."
"Oh."
We went out on the street. Alice looked at the crowd over near the subway exit. Distantly, a siren wailed.
She pulled at my arm. "Let's go over."
"It ain't smart."
"Just this one time. Please."
"All right, Alice. But you're pushing too hard."
A sweating traffic cop was trying to get things organized. "Move along," he urged. "There's nothing to see. Keep moving."
"Has there been an accident, Officer?" Alice asked, innocently.
The cop must have been surprised by a voice coming from the shapeless, milling crowd. He answered, "Some joker got himself shot." Then, realizing he'd said too much, "Keep it moving, I said. This ain't a sideshow."
As we circled around the fat man's body, Alice's fingers tightened on my arm.
"Fred—I feel so . . . tingly. It's just like sex."
"Shut up."
She squoze me again. "Look at him!"
Someone, probably the cop, had spread a handkerchief over the fat man's face. It was clotted and stiff with blood. As for his body, it was only cotton stuffing crammed into the shiny blue suit, nothing but a rag doll all limp and boneless.
"Come on," I said. "We seen enough. Let's go home."
When we got there, Alice climbed all over me before we got into the bedroom.

OFF DUTY COP SLAIN
BY PICKPOCKET

Sergeant Marvin Miller, 41, an 18-year veteran of the New York Police Department, was shot and killed last night at Lincoln Center, apparently while attempting to apprehend a pickpocket. Miller was found clutching a wallet, which had been stolen just moments before from Mrs. Henry Pope, the Bronx. Miller was killed by a bullet wound made with a .22 caliber pistol fired into his head at close range.

"This is another example of the tragedy caused by traffic in illegal handguns," said the mayor in a press conference at Gracie Mansion. "Those so-called Saturday Night Specials, which are easily available in a number of southern states, particularly Florida, where, as you know, I was viciously attacked by the press for condemning their sale, find their way onto the modern-day 'underground railroad' and into the hands of urban criminals. This traffic must and will be halted."

The mayor went on to call for tougher federal gun control laws.

Police Commissioner Samuel

Jackson promised a thorough investigation and predicted an
early arrest.

"We have information that we
aren't revealing," said the commissioner. "It may be that Sergeant Miller was working on
something undercover. There's
more to this case than a simple
pickpocket charge."

"Cops!" I said. "When you don't want one, they're all
over the place, even picking people's pockets."

Worried, Alice said, "He *did* steal that wallet. We
saw him."

"Don't you fret none, Alice. We got the right feller.
He just happened to be a cop who picked up a few
extra bucks moonlighting as a pickpocket."

Alice stared at her fingertips. "It's funny," she said
softly. "Last night feels so long ago. Now it seems like
such a small reason for a man to die . . . just for stealing a woman's wallet."

"Big woman, you sure changed your tune suddenly,"
I said. "Last night you was so hot to trot that you
couldn't hardly wait to bring one of them down. And
now it sounds like you're feeling *sorry* for him."

"That was before," she said. "It's all . . . different,
now. I don't seem to feel the same bitterness I had toward everybody. It's as if the debt has been paid."

"Well, hooray for you," I said. "Now that you're
happy again, I suppose you'd like to call the whole
thing off."

"I didn't say that. But, yes, if you want the truth, it

does seem excessive, taking a man's life for something as minor as purse snatching."

"Lady, I told you before, there ain't no such thing as minor crimes. I put up with a lot, and they kept coming after me and mine, and when they got to you that finished it, and I decided to put my foot down. I ain't asking for your advice now that it's too late to put the clock back. This thing is started, and it ain't going to finish until *I* say it's finished. You got that, Alice?"

She kissed me. "I know you did it for me, and I know that someone has to do something. But why does it have to be you? I'm worried. I don't want you to get in trouble over me."

"You stay to home from now on when I go out, and there won't be no trouble."

She folded her hands. "All right. I'll do whatever you say, Fred."

So that ended that. I maybe should have had better sense than to even let her know what I was planning, much less take her along. I learned a long time ago that it's bad news to go in business with someone you're related to or mixed up with, and that includes the business of shooting down folks. And if it's a woman you're taking in with you, it's double trouble. You can't give them hell when they do a bad job because they take it personal and get all upset. You find yourself doing stuff over yourself rather than asking them to do it right. No, take it from Fred Frederickson, don't ever open up shop with your wife or your girl friend.

The next time I went out, I left Alice in the apartment. I didn't even tell her I was going. I just sneaked the Halliburton case from the closet and slipped out like a tippytoe churchmouse.

When I got back, she was frantic.

"You've been gone for hours!" she said. Her eyes was red. "I was positive something had happened to you. Why didn't you tell me you were going?"

I handed her the gun case and said, "Put it away. And make me a drink."

She stashed the gun and poured me a shot of Jack Daniels. She gave it to me and said, "Did you . . . ?"

"Got two."

She sat down on the floor and rested her head against my knee.

"Tell me," she whispered.

"They was these two black fellers over on Columbus Avenue. They won't be missed. There's plenty left. After the shots, the niggers came out of the buildings like cockroaches."

Alice winced. "Do you have to call them *that*?"

"Well, hon, there sure were a *lot* of them."

"I meant the other."

"Nigger? Alice, *you* ain't going to start on me too, are you? I heard you call them that your very own self."

"Only when I was angry and upset."

"Well, big woman, I don't mean no insult, but sometimes my tongue slips. Hell, nigger's what I always heard them called as long as I can remember. Back in Kansas City, there was even a rodeo rider called himself Nigger Jack. He seemed right proud of the name."

"You shouldn't use it," she said.

"Do you want to hear what happened, or do you want to turn on the TV set and watch them Bonanza fellers?"

"I want you to tell me what you did," she said.

"Okay," I said. "But hush up with the side comments."

I went out on one of the actual roofs this time, and you can believe that it was cold when the wind hit me. I ducked down in the shadow of a chimney. I didn't worry about nobody coming out and finding me there. I had me a bicycle lock with a flexible steel cable, and I'd wrapped it around the doorknob and fastened it so the roof door couldn't be opened from the inside.

I glassed up and down Columbus Avenue for maybe ten minutes before I saw what I was looking for.

One of those Ford Econoline vans drove up and a husky white man got out and went inside the bar on the corner. He locked up the van before he left, but he made one big mistake—he left one of the little sliding back windows ajar.

The black boy, a tall, skinny one around twenty years old, came out of the shadows so fast I almost didn't see him. He snaked his arm through the open window, unlatched the front door, and slipped inside, all in a matter of seconds. He was no amateur; you could see right off he'd done this kind of work before.

I opened up the case and took out the rifle and clicked on the skeleton stock. When I laid it over the edge of the roof, I could see inside the van real easy

199

through the four-power Weaver scope. The thief was laying down on the front seat, working under the dashboard.

I slid a round in the chamber and waited. I didn't want to bust no innocent driver's front window if I had a choice.

It only took him a couple of minutes to finish what he was doing, and then he come out of the van holding an expensive tape deck close to his body. He looked up and down the street to see if anybody had been watching. Four or five had, but they didn't seem to mind. One gave him a clenched-fist-in-the-air salute and turned away.

The thief's eyes was sparkling white in the neon glow. I laid the cross hairs right between them and squoze the trigger.

His head blew up like a big black punkin with a cherry bomb inside it.

Two more come out of the shadows. They looked around, mumbling to each other. They peered down at the fallen boy, called out to him, moved closer when there was no answer.

I watched through the field glasses as they bent over. When they saw the blood, they jumped back and both of them run inside a doorway.

I had started to dismantle the rifle when a furtive motion caught my eye.

One of them had sneaked back out on the sidewalk. His hand dipped into the dead boy's pocket and slipped out a wallet. It vanished into his jacket. Then he pried the tape deck loose from the dead fingers and started back into the shadows with it.

I slid another round into the chamber. When he stood up with the tape deck, I had the cross hairs dead center on his head. He was turning away when I fired, because just after rifle went *pffft!* I heard the slug hit him, and it must have taken him in solid bone instead of the forehead. A big chunk of his head went flying straight up in the air, tumbling and letting the shattered skull flash white against the street light's glare.

He tumbled forward into the shadows and didn't move, not even a twitch.

Now people started running out of the buildings. The more that came, the more there seemed to be. They mumbled among themselves and looked all around the street, and when some of them started looking up at the rooftops, I figured it was time to make tracks.

I packed the gun and went down the five flights of urine-stained stairs carefully, not making any noise.

Outside, the street was jammed with people, mostly black. I saw the van's driver come out of the corner bar.

"Hey," he yelled, "that's my tape deck!"

He bent over to pick it up, but two black men pushed him back. He made a fuss, and they started beating up on him, one holding while the other hit.

I started for the far corner. Three black youths barred my way.

"Where you think you goin', old man?"

"What's yo' hurry?" said another.

"What you got in that suitcase? Looks like it might be a camera."

"Or maybe one of them little Sony TV's?"

I held the Halliburton case lightly in my left hand. My weight was poised on the ball of one foot. If they got a little closer, I would kick the first one in the nuts, brain the second with the heavy aluminum case, and then have both hands free to dispose of the last one at my pleasure. It might even be fun. It's all right to shoot some bastard from a distance, but there ain't nothing quite like getting your hands on him.

"Back off there," said a new voice. Two cops, fierce in their hard hats, had come up behind me.

The three blacks scattered and ran.

"This ain't no place for you, old-timer," said one of the cops. "Better find another street. You could get hurt on this one."

"You ain't just bird-turding," I said in my old man's voice. "Thankee kindly, boys."

"Don't mention it," said the cop as he and his buddy moved into the angry crowd, hands held close to the squat butts of their service revolvers.

TWO SLAIN AS GANG WAR SHATTERS NEIGHBORHOOD PEACE

Violence errupted last night on Columbus Avenue when two rival neighborhood gangs shot it out with zip guns. The two "clubs"—The Young Turks and the 84th Street Eagles—had been observing an uneasy truce arranged by Job Corps mediators.

Both victims were slain with zip guns—homemade pistols constructed from lengths of pipe and rubber bands, firing a single .22 cartridge.

The melee apparently began when two young men clashed over a tape deck that had fallen from a passing truck. The truck's driver was reported in Roosevelt Hospital with head injuries sustained when he fell from the moving vehicle.

No arrests were made, but an investigation is under way, according to the mayor's office.

"It's amazing!" Alice said. "They managed to get every single fact wrong. Nobody has any idea what's really happening. You've shot three men so far and to this moment, nobody's even got a clue that their deaths weren't the result of normal crime violence."

"I ain't sure that's so good," I said.

"Why not? If they aren't looking for you, they can't catch you."

I was cleaning the rifle's bore with a cloth patch soaked with Hoppe's nitrate solvent. I held the gun up and squinted through the barrel. It was clean and shiny.

"I know," I said. "But if nobody knows what I'm up to, what *good* will it do?"

"Well, at least those two won't steal any more tape decks."

"No, but somebody else will, because they ain't had no warning about what'll happen to them if they do. Alice, I didn't just set out to pay people off. I want them to learn not to come after us, to stay the hell away from me and mine. You want the truth, girl, I don't give a solitary shit what happens to some stupid truck driver and his tape deck. It serves him right for not locking up good. But I don't want any of those bastards ever busting down your door again to get at your TV set."

"Well," Alice said, "I don't think they're getting the message."

"They will," I said. "I'll make damned sure they get it."

I wouldn't want it said that I was only shooting cops and niggers, because that wasn't so. I didn't blast down them last two because they was black, but because they was *bad*. Much as I disapprove of most cops, old Fatty hadn't got his head blown off for being one, but for being a pickpocket. All I do is put the bullet where the blame is.

Well, anyway, you can see how I had to find me a target a little more important in the scheme of things, so I decided to go out in broad daylight, down to Madison Avenue, where there ought to be a better class of crook.

It was a working day, and the streets was all crowded,

and I had me a hard time finding a place to set up shop. But finally I located a spot behind a pile of lumber where they was putting up a new skyscraper. The way I figure it, this here New York City is going to be real nice if they ever finish building it.

There was a few bad moments when six construction workers sat down practically on top of my head and started eating lunch. But then some pretty girls come along, and they all run out on the sidewalk to hoot and holler and whistle. I crept over to one side, so when they come back there wouldn't be no chance of them seeing me, and played dead until the whistle blew and they went back to work. Then I snuck back to my first position and waited.

I spotted my target through a store window, and for a minute, I thought I'd made a mistake. He sure didn't look like anybody who ought to be laid low. But I didn't even need my field glasses to see that this quiet, good-looking feller with steel-gray hair at his temples and a two-hundred-dollar suit on his back, was a plain old thief. He waited until the tobacco shop salesman had his back turned, and then he reached over, slick as a whistle, and stole a ten-dollar pipe.

Now, I knew what Alice would have said if she was here. A ten-dollar pipe just ain't worth a man's life. But if *it* ain't, what is? Where are you going to draw the line? This feller was just as much of a thief as if he'd took out a pistol and held up the corner bank. And while I had to admit there was less chance of *him* ever coming after me and mine and causing us misery, he was part of the whole mess and besides, like I said before, I needed me an example that nobody could blame on a gang rumble.

He came out of the tobacco shop whistling happily and stopped at the corner, waiting for the light to change. With a sly smile, he took out the pipe and admired it.

He went happy, I'll tell you that, because at that very second I exploded his brains.

He fell down in the street and a surprised bus driver run over him before he could get the Number 21 bus stopped.

To The Editor —

I heard on the Late News how that feller on Madison avenue got hit by a bus and that just aint so. I sure hope you folks set the story straight in your newspaper. That man was shot, and if you look close, you'll find the bullet, so go tell them cops they're barking up the wrong tree.

A. Friend

SNIPER SLAYS VICTIM
ON MADISON AVENUE

A sniper's bullet claimed the life of Stuart McIlroy, 51, prominent Madison Avenue accountant, during yesterday's lunch hour rush, police announced today.

At first, Mr. McIlroy's death was attributed to a traffic accident, but acting on information provided by this newspaper, the coroner's office discovered the fatal bullet wound.

Although the bullet was completely shattered, police gave their opinion that it was one of the sophisticated missiles developed for use in the Vietnam conflict, probably a Mazzi .29 millimeter high-spiral random-impact bullet, commonly called "The Tumbler" by CIA snipers who developed it for political assassinations.

Contacted in Washington, a high source said, "I don't know how one of these weapons could have fallen into private hands. They are very sophisticated, you know, with radar aiming and heat-seeking ballistics."

Working in cooperation with investigators, this newspaper provided the original clue that revealed what may have been

the latest in a long—and pre-
viously undetected—series of
sniper murders.

Reached at her suburban
Westchester home, Mrs. McIlroy
denied that her husband had
been doing secret government
work and sobbed, "I just don't
know anyone who would have
done this terrible thing. He was
such a good man."

I threw the newspaper down.

"I'll be a dirty name! Mazzi random-impact my ass!
And they took my letter and give it to the cops instead
of printing it like I wanted. Now they got a sample of
my handwriting and the folks out there *still* don't
know what the hell this is all about."

Alice didn't seem to care. She was staring at the newspaper. "Did you read it all?" she asked. "It's awful. He
had four children. One is mentally retarded. That poor
woman—what's she going to do?"

"He should have thought about them before he stole
that pipe," I said. "Lay off, Alice. If you're going to fuss
and nag at me every time I do a job, I'll just stop telling you about them."

"Maybe that wouldn't bother me," she said.

I didn't pay her no mind. "I got to figure out a way
to reach the *people*," I said. "Hell, if *they* don't know,
what's the point in it all? You know what we need, big
woman? Something like them Deep Balm commercials.
Now folks knew *they* was around."

I stopped. "Hell, yes!" I said.

"What are you thinking about?" Alice asked.

"Well, we can't make no TV commercial. It costs too much, and even if it didn't, we'd have to let too many people in on what we're doing. No, TV is out. But how about radio, big woman? We can do that ourselves, and it won't cost hardly nothing."

"How?"

I handed her some money. "Go down to the Korvette store and buy me one of them little cassette tape recorders. They don't cost more than thirty, forty dollars."

"What are you going to use it for?"

"You'll see. Just do what I said."

So she did.

ANNOUNCER: The time, at the tone, exactly eight P.M.

SFX: Time tone.

ANNOUNCER: WBRZ, listener-supported radio, 104.6 on your FM dial. And now, the Skip Mitchell Show.

SKIP: Skip Mitchell here with "Sounds of the City." East side, west side, all around the town, our portable microphone brings you the pulse of New York.

Tonight, a unique and terrifying adventure in sound. For perhaps the first time on any radio program, the actual sound of murder.

This is no joke, folks. You are going to hear a man really being killed. And you'll hear the self-confessed murderer explaining his action. You'll have to forgive the substandard audio quality, you hi-fi enthusiasts. The master recording was made on a home-quality cassette recorder, and you know what *that* means. The cassette was dropped into our mail chute sometime this morning, by a person or persons unknown. When we played the tape, at first we thought it was a hoax, but then we decided to call the police, and they confirmed that the murder described actually *did* take place last night in Greenwich Village. I might add that they demanded we turn the cassette over to them so they could run voice-print ID checks and, in the interests of law and order, we did so. However, also in the interests of a free press and your right to immediate access to the news, we made a dupe before we released the cassette to the fuzz . . . sorry, men. The police. They'll probably flip their wigs over this, but you, the listener, have a right—and if what that man on the tape says is so—a real *need* to hear this recording.

So, to all you off-the-air tape hijackers, start your reels turning now . . . and listen to the sound of murder.

(PAUSE)

MAN: How does this goddamned thing work?

WOMAN: It's recording now. You have to push this red button.

MAN: Oh, yeah, I see the tape moving. Okay. Listen, you people. I been shooting folks because they been doing wrong, and coming after me and mine. But so far, the stupid cops have dropped the ball and they ain't figured out what the hell's going on. Well, it's to your best interests to know what's happening, because if you don't and you go out and you do something wrong, why I'm just liable to shoot *you* too, and that would be a pity. So just listen to me real close.

The first one I shot, back on Monday night, he was a cop, but that ain't why I shot him. He was hanging around Lincoln Center, snitching wallets out of women's purses. I seen him take one, so I shot him. The stupid cops, they said he got killed trying to capture a pickpocket. Well, ain't that a caution? *He* was the pickpocket, nobody else, and he ought to have known better, and then he wouldn't be pushing up daisies.

Tuesday night, I went up to Eighty-fourth Street and Columbus Avenue, and shot me a nigger because he stole a tape deck out of a truck. And that's *why* I shot him, not because he was black, but because he was a thief. Then another nigger come out, and he started stealing from the first one I'd shot, so naturally, I shot *him* too. Well, if you saw the newspapers, you know the stupid cops said those two fellers got killed in a gang war with zip guns. Zip guns? Who the hell are they trying to fool? Anybody knows you can't hardly even *hit* nobody with one of them homemade guns, let alone shoot two boys in their heads and scramble their brains.

Then on Wednesday, I went down to Madison Avenue and shot me a big wheel accountant on account of how he shoplifted a ten-dollar pipe from the Bright Leaf Tobacco Shoppe. He was a nice-looking gentleman, and I hated to do it, but what's fair for one is fair for all.

Do you think the stupid cops finally got on the ball? Like hell they did. They said that poor man got hisself killed by a bus, for Christ's sake, and it was only because I got mad and wrote a letter to the newspaper that they ever did check careful and find out how that feller had been shot. But the newspaper tried to take all the credit, and they didn't print none of my letter, so I figured out this way to let you folks know how things are going to be from now on in this city. I'm just getting ready to go down to Greenwich Village, on account of there's always something bad happening down there, and if this machine's working right, I'll let

> you hear what happens. So you just wait until I start
> talking again.

(PAUSE)

How do you turn this goddamned thing off?

WOMAN: The red button.

MAN: Oh, yeah.

(VERY LONG PAUSE)

SFX: Street noises, mingled with distant rock music.

MAN: . . . throw this goddamned thing out the window. I guess it's working now. I can see the tape moving anyways. Shit, I let one get away while I was trying to get this fu——(BLEEP) thing working.

> Like I said, I come down here to Greenwich Village, and I got me a spot on top of an old brownstone overlooking MacDougal Street. It's a good thing I don't consider smoking marijuana a crime, because I could have shot me at least a dozen potheads so far, standing right out in the open down there puffing away. I can smell it all the way up here on the roof.

> The one that got away, he tried to get some girl to give him some money, and when she wouldn't, he whaled the living shit out of her. I'd of got him sure, but I was trying to make this stupid machine work, and he got inside out of range before I could line him up.

> Now, if you'll just listen careful, this is what it sounds like when I feed a round into the chamber.

SFX: Click of rifle bolt.

MAN: Okay, we're loaded up now. While we're waiting for something to happen, I'll try to explain why I'm doing all this.

It ain't that I honestly believe the city is the Devil's Playground, but you got to admit, you city people sure as hell cause more trouble than you're worth. Most times, I would have just walked off and let you stew in your own fat. But you made the mistake of jumping on both me *and* my woman, and your Law, it just sat by and did nothing, except when it was trying to punish *us* because we wouldn't be nice quiet victims and lay down and die without fussing. If you think I aim to let you get away with that, you got another think coming.

By the time I'm through, you're going to be nice and friendly, or you're going to be dead. Is that clear enough for you?

Hold on there, I think we got us one. He's a tall man, in a good suit. He looks like one of them Italians. Some of them hippie kids is giving him the eye. Now they're going over to talk with him.

Yes sir, I was right. That feller's dealing dope. He sold them kids two little envelopes full of white powder. You all just excuse me for a minute.

(PAUSE)

SFX: *Sprang!*

SFX: Crowd hubbub. Woman's scream.

(PAUSE)

MAN: Sorry, folks, I forgot you was listening. Well, what happened there was, I got so distracted worrying about this cassette recorder picking up everything I said that I didn't hold too steady when I squoze off. Hell, to be honest, I probably flinched. Anyway, instead of taking him in the head like I wanted, I got that dope peddler right in the Adam's apple. He slammed back against a streetlight post and started grabbing at his shirt front, plucking the cloth away in big white hand-

213

fuls. His throat looked like an old-fashioned gooseneck pump, spurting red a good six feet out into the street. I couldn't hear him up here, but you could see that our boy made himself some noise. Then he bent over and dove head first right in the back seat of a passing sports car. The driver practically had a shit hemorrhage. Now, if you'll excuse me again, I guess I better pack up my gear and clear out of here. There ain't no doubt *this* one got shot, and they might start checking out the roofs.

(PAUSE)

Well, I played back this here tape, and I want to finish up what I was saying.

Like I said, a man who'd steal a pipe from a store'd steal from me. And I just ain't going to let him do it. Not anymore. A feller who'd break into a truck would break into my house. And I ain't going to give *him* the chance, neither. You all have got to get it in your heads that you can't come after me no more, because I done give up sitting still for it.

Now, you ain't in no trouble unless you go out looking for it. I ain't one of them crazy snipers shooting at anything that moves. You keep your hands in your own pockets, don't open anyone's car door but your own, don't push other folks in the face, and you ain't got a single thing to worry about. But keep on grabbing and pushing and I guarantee you, one fine day you'll end up missing your head. Because we'll get you, Alice and me.

SKIP: Well, that's the tape, listeners. The most amazing, terrifying, weird experience I've ever had in radio. As I said, the police have confiscated the original cassette, and I'm sure we'll be hearing from them for daring to make this broadcast. But, frankly, I don't agree with Police Commissioner Jackson, that his message, frightening and deranged though it might be, should be kept secret. After all, it's *your* lives that are being threatened.

Hey, I just had a crazy idea. Why not do what this crazy says? Call a moratorium on stealing and hurting each other—and nobody'll get shot!

Alice was horrified when we heard the program. "You told them my name!"

"No I didn't."

" 'We'll get you, Alice and me.' That's what you said."

I scratched my head. "Guess I did, at that. Well, it was just a little slip."

"Little for *you*. They can't trace you because you referred to yourself as 'me.' But my name is Alice, and what's more, you left in all that stuff at the beginning where I told you how to operate the machine. Now they've got voice print samples of *both* of us."

"I guess maybe they do."

"Doesn't it *bother* you!"

"Not very much. They got to catch us before them voice-prints, whatever they are, is worth the paper they're printed on. And they ain't going to catch us."

"But what if they do?"

"Like I said, hon, you don't get no guarantee on to-morrow."

She couldn't hide how scared she was. "I think you ought to stop, Fred."

"Why?"

She stared down at her hands. "Because we're going to get caught. And besides, suddenly it seems all *wrong*."

"What's wrong about stopping folks from stealing and killing?"

"But *are* you stopping them?"

"Not yet. But that radio show ought to help. They can't sweep us under the rug now. Too many people heard the truth."

"Don't be too sure about that," said Alice.

RADIO STATION SUED FOR SLANDER

Controversial FM radio station WBRZ, one of the so-called listener-supported noncommercial operations, was named as co-defendent in a $3,000,000 lawsuit brought today by Mrs. Ann McIlroy, widow of accountant Stuart McIlroy, who was slain last week on Madison Avenue by a sniper's bullet.

Named as primary defendant in the action was Marvin ("Skip") Mitchell, host of a program called "Sounds of the City."

Mrs. McIlroy's attorney declared, "Mr. Mitchell and station WBRZ acted in the poorest taste by slandering Mrs. McIlroy's deceased husband before his coffin was even in the ground. In the guise of a radio documentary, which police have branded as a hoax, Mr. Mitchell and WBRZ made serious allegations against the late Mr. McIlroy which, had he lived, would have seriously damaged his reputation and standing in the community. These allegations have adversely affected his widow. We do not intend to let such irresponsible statements pass unchallenged."

Mr. Mitchell was unavailable for comment, although a source close to City Hall revealed that the broadcaster was undergoing intensive questioning by the district attorney's office.

"Holy shit!" I said. "Here they've gone and locked that poor bastard up just for playing my tape! What the hell do I have to do to make them believe me?"

"I don't think you ought to do anything," Alice said. "Fred, how many times do I have to tell you, I feel bad about this whole thing? I wish you'd stop!"

"Wish away," I said. "But I ain't *ready* to stop. Those bastards out there ain't *heard* me yet. What I done so far ain't had no more effect on them than shooting a BB into the ocean."

"And that's all the effect you'll ever have," she said. "It's too big for you, Fred. You can't change ten million people just by killing a few of them. There's too many of them. They don't even notice."

"They're *going* to notice," I said, taking the Halliburton case out of the closet.

"Fred! What are you going to do?"

"It's twelve noon now. I'm going to get me one an hour until midnight."

"Fred!"

I slammed the door.

Ten minutes later, I found me a mugger in Riverside Park. I scrambled his brains, and his old lady victim took off, running and hollering like a teen-ager.

Then I got me a cat burglar. I saw him creeping down a fire escape. He pried open a window, slipped inside, and come out carrying a portable TV. I dropped him, and felt a little sorry when the TV set smashed on the sidewalk.

I got lucky over on West End Avenue and nailed me two hippies who was breaking into a station wagon. One of them was a girl, and when she fell, her skirt slipped up around her waist and she didn't have no panties on. Some little Puerto Rican kid stood there staring at her pussy and that made me so mad that I almost wanted to shoot him, too. But even if I didn't like it, what he was doing wasn't no crime, so I let him go.

Twelve blocks away, a punk kid hit an old man with a beer bottle, and I hit him with a .22 slug.

Then I dropped a nigger whore on Ninety-sixth Street for swiping a John's wallet when she poured him into a taxi. And right across the street, a punk pulled a switchblade on a taxi driver and tried to pry out his lock box, so I dropped *him,* too.

218

By now, I could hear at least a dozen sirens converging on the West Side, so I got on the subway and went on down to Wall Street. On the way, I got a tall blond boy who was jostling the passengers and stealing their wallets. I waited for him between the cars and blasted him from less than two inches away, and he fell down under the wheels.

Wall Street was a little quieter, but I still found me a purse snatcher. He wasn't as slick as the first fat man had been. He just grabbed a strap and took off like a bat out of hell, but I was up on a roof, and got him as he ran in front of the U.S. Customs building. Then I collected me a sailor who was beating up on some undernourished hooker. He fell down in her arms and, stupidly, she tried to hold him up and screamed and screamed. . . .

That made nine, and it wasn't even five in the afternoon yet. I was doing pretty good. And my shooting was better, too. I had my eye back. I'd hit all nine right smack in the head.

I picked up my last three in Central Park, because it commenced to get hot down around Wall Street, too. It sounded like a million air-raid sirens were going off. I found me one bastard slugging a little kid. He may have been the kid's father, because the kid took on something awful after I dropped him. But father or not, what he was doing was assault. And I got me a dude with a gravity knife who was doing a little cutting on a skinny black boy, and finally, a big fat woman who was walking quietly down the row of gossiping nannies, grouped along the benches with their expensive baby carriages. Without breaking stride, she was picking up their purses, one by one.

Then I went home. It had been a long day, and I was tired.

CRAZED SNIPER HOLDS
CITY AT BAY

At least twelve men and women were slain from ambush yesterday by a sniper who declared, in an exclusive communication with this newspaper, that he was acting to replace the law, which according to him, "Don't work no more."

According to a letter written by the sniper and delivered to this newspaper, the victims were all slain while in the act of committing such "crimes" as mugging, burglary, assault, and theft.

Police admitted reluctantly that at least "some" of the victims may have been engaged in illegal activities shortly before being shot down.

Police Commissioner Jackson has placed his department on 24-hour alert. All vacations have been canceled and overtime has been authorized for several precincts in congested areas.

The commissioner denied

that the FBI had been called in to assist during the emergency.

"Our men are among the nation's finest," he said. "They'll handle this matter efficiently and without delay."

The commissioner expressed confidence that an arrest would be made "soon."

(Please turn to page 31 for an important editorial)

TO THE SNIPER,
WHOEVER YOU ARE
PLEASE READ THIS!

This newspaper has received your letters and agrees with you in principle that public morality has reached a deplorable low. We agree that something must be done.

But you're going at it the wrong way!

Killing isn't the answer.

That you chose it indicates you're in need of help.

Let us help you.

Don't use your gun again. That won't solve anything.

Instead, call Harvey Bush, managing editor of this newspaper, any time, day or night. He's standing by to hear from you.

We promise to help you receive fair and humane treatment. We promise to help deliver your message to the people of New York City. Our pages are at your disposal.

Wouldn't it be better to try to change people with sound, rational discussion, instead of bloodshed?

We know you'll agree with us if only you will sit down and remember for a moment the most important of the Ten Commandments.

Thou shalt not kill.

Please call us now. We're waiting to help you.

"They're waiting to put me in jail," I told Alice. "Or better yet, the booby hatch."

She didn't answer. She hadn't done much talking since I got home last night and told her I'd gotten my round dozen.

Now, ain't that enough to sour your bile? Here I only went in this shooting business on account of her, and if you remember, she was mighty hot to trot that first time. Then, all of a sudden, she goes and gets religion.

I'll tell you, I was just about disgusted enough to give up the whole mess.

Only thing, like I said, I like to leave my campgrounds cleaner than I found them. And *any* change I could bring about here in the city was bound to be an improvement. I hated to give up before I saw *some* results.

But when a woman goes sour, all the fun goes out of life. You can't talk to her without fighting because she takes everything the wrong way. You can't enjoy your meals because, deliberate or not, she'll burn your meat when you like it red, or put club soda in your whiskey instead of tap water. Even the screwing ain't no fun. She'll make a big thing out of "giving in" to you and lay there with about as much energy as a board with a fur-lined knot hole.

"Fred," she said, "you've got to stop."

"I ain't ready to stop," I said. "I got today's twelve quicker than you'd imagine. They ain't learned one goddamned thing. They're as busy as a hive of bees out there, stealing, fighting and all the rest."

Later, I heard her get up in the darkness and, crouching in the closet, count my boxes of ammo.

She didn't come back to bed, but slept on the couch, and that was fine with me.

IN THE NAME OF GOD
DON'T KILL ANYMORE!

Please heed this message!

During the past week, more than fifty lives have been extinguished by your "avenging" rifle.

Isn't that enough?

Our offer to help you still stands. Call us anytime. Our switchboard has instructions to relay your call to Mr. Bush wherever he may be, day or night. Your call will not be

monitored and we promise to
make no attempt to trace it.
In God's name, stop the killing!

"Fred," Alice said, "listen to them. Please."

"No, ma'am. Not until I see some results."

Her lips tightened. "Then I'll turn you in myself. I
swear it."

"Suit yourself. You know where the telephone is.
Meanwhile, I'm going to bed. A man gets tired, climbing up and down on them roofs."

I woke up once during the night and heard her
crying in the darkness.

EIGHTEEN

Well, I told you how it is when the fun goes out of something. Every day for more than a week I went out and got my dozen, but it didn't give me no pleasure, it was just flat and dull like doing your duty because you have to, not because you want to. Alice wouldn't even talk to me no more.

The only thing that kept me from packing up was that it finally looked like I was getting results. Every day it got harder and harder to pick up my dozen. One reason was, there was fewer people on the streets. Folks seemed to be staying inside more these days. But even those that was out seemed to be behaving themselves better.

"One more week," I promised Alice, trying to break down that wall she'd built up between us. "That's all the time I'll need to be sure the job's done right. Next Friday we'll head for the high country."

"Pack up and go alone, old man," she said. "I've traveled as far on this crazy trip of yours as I care to."

"Well, goody on you," I said. "While you're at it, why don't you call up The Law and get rid of me for once and all?"

Flatly, she said, "I would, except I'm afraid they'd lock me up, too. All I can hope is that they shoot you down like you deserve." She stared at me defiantly. "So now you know."

"Couldn't be plainer," I said. "It's sad, ain't it, the way things had to come down to a sorry pass like this. I honestly only set out to try and please you, Alice, but it all went wrong."

"That's right," she said. "Blame it on me. It's *my* fault all those people are dead."

"I wasn't trying to blame nothing on you, Alice. But I guess that's how you know things are really over, ain't it? When all there is to share is blame?"

She didn't answer. I got up and took the Halliburton case out of the closet. "Time to go to work," I said.

She came after me. Every time she sucked in a breath, it made a ragged, tearing sound in the back of her throat. "Stop it, Fred! Admit it, the only reason you've done this is because you *enjoy* killing people!"

I thought about what she'd said. "No," I said slowly. "That ain't so. I don't enjoy it, at least not like I enjoy a good meal, or a cool drink, or a warm night in bed. Though it's got to please a man a little when he does his job good."

"I should have realized it sooner," she said. "You're crazy. And for a while there, you had *me* crazy too. It all started that evening in Washington Square, when you nearly killed those two boys. Why, you didn't even think of them as being human beings."

"Well, was they? They come after me, didn't they? I told you a dozen times, Alice, *nobody* comes after me or mine. And that's what those two boys did, and that's what Mary Lou did, and that's what this whole goddamned *city* did, and I won't tolerate it."

Alice sank down in the big armchair in front of the fancy color TV set that we never watched anymore.

"I was right," she said, so low I almost couldn't hear her. "My God, why didn't I see it before?"

"Alice, honey, I got me a lot of running around and climbing to do today, so if you ain't going to turn me in to The Law, I've got to get moving."

"I should," she said, her voice muffled. "But how can I?"

CITY CRIME RATE PLUMMETS TO NEW LOW

Apparently deterred by the sniper whose high-powered rifle has claimed more than some dozen lives a day in the past three weeks, criminals and petty lawbreakers have gone into virtual retirement, resulting in the city's lowest crime rate in recorded history.

A confidential source, who admits privately to a series of night burglaries, stated it this way: "That guy is bananas. He'll

shoot you just for making an illegal left turn. It ain't worth getting shot just to heist a sewing
machine. I'm leaving town, and
so are a lot of my buddies. It's
too hot here."

Oddly enough, the ordinary
citizen seemed to accept the situ-
ation calmly.

A plumber from Queens said,
"I never had it so good. I don't
even bother to lock my truck up
anymore. Who's going to take a
chance on getting a bullet in the
head just to swipe ten bucks
worth of pipe?" And, after a nervous laugh, "Meanwhile, I
admit, I'm being a lot more
accurate on my estimates."

A Black humanities student
at NYU said, "This cat's got it
all together. He ain't shot no
one who ain't been doing something wrong. That was kind of
hard on the first poor guy who
got wasted for stealing hubcaps,
but after the word got out, nobody has to worry about their
hubcaps anymore."

Meanwhile, the mayor denied
that the Mafia has put a $10,000
price on the sniper's head. Otherwise, at City Hall, the most
frequent statement given report-
ers has been, "No comment."

But officials finally admitted

that agents of the FBI were
working on the case under the
federal presumption that those
killed in the commission of
crimes had been denied a fair
trial and deprived of their civil
rights.

President Howard Foster
evaded the issue at his monthly
press conference, calling it "a
local matter under the control of
local Republican officials." President Foster, of course, is a Dem-
ocrat.

Meanwhile, as night ap-
proaches again, New York City
waits, asking the question:
Who will be next?

"You're hurt!" Alice screamed, as I let myself in. She
ran to me. For a moment, our anger and disagreements
seemed forgotten.

"It ain't as bad as it looks," I said. "I'm mostly just
tuckered out."

"What happened? You're bleeding."

"It's just a graze."

She put a damp towel against my head. "Did someone shoot you?"

"Fix me a drink first, baby."

She poured me a double bourbon. I sipped at it and
got my breath back.

"*Tell* me, Fred!"

"Well, I sat on this one roof up in Harlem for almost
two hours," I said. . . .

. . . and it was cold there with the wind blowing, and no action down in the streets even worth unlatching the case for.

What you got to do is settle in your mind what's important, and *who's* important, and to hell with the rest of them.

It sure seemed clear and logical to me. So why in hell was Alice saying I was *crazy?*

Just then, I saw me a target. He was a little Mexican, or maybe he was one of them Puerto Ricans. He was backed up against the locked door of a cigar store. He had his hands behind his back, and he was moving them kind of funny.

I assembled the rifle, charged the chamber, and waited. I'd of bet you anything he was picking the lock.

Sure enough, the door of the store started to ease open behind him.

I lifted the rifle.

"Freeze!" yelled a voice, off to my left.

I've seen that TV show too often not to know what that means. Over there somewhere in the shadows was an FBI man and he'd be holding his revolver with two hands. If they followed the TV script, he'd only shoot me in the leg, because on that show they make it look like the FBI never shoots to kill, but me, I don't believe everything I see on TV.

I made a dive off to the right, behind a chimney, and sure enough a bullet plowed up the asphalt roofing just where my head had been. As I rolled, I swung the rifle barrel around and when it was lined up with a man crouched behind a ventilator stack, I squoze off a round and it busted him right between the eyes. I jacked another shell into the chamber in case there were two of them, but nothing else moved, so I grabbed my aluminum case and got the hell out of there. . . .

While I told her what happened, Alice sat there quietly, listening. One hand was pressed against her mouth.

"You killed him?" she whispered. "An FBI man?"

"How do I know he was FBI? He might have been one of them pistoleros the Mafia sent out to get me."

"He *must* have been FBI," she said. "Otherwise he wouldn't have called out a warning. Oh, Fred, you've done it now."

"You might be right. But that's the first mistake I've made in two hundred and forty-one shots. That ain't too bad."

"The others were terrible enough, but at least you might say you had some sort of justification, they were committing crimes. But this man was only doing his duty."

"His duty was concerned mostly with putting a bullet through my head. There didn't seem to be no future in letting him do that."

"Why didn't you give yourself up?"

"And let them shove me in the hoosegow? I thought you figured that was the worst thing that could happen to a body."

"You're right," she said softly. "No matter what you've done, I couldn't let them put you *there*. Oh, Fred, why didn't you go away when you could? Now it's too late."

"I don't see why. Things ain't really changed. That feller up there won't do no talking. The Law still ain't got no idea on earth who or where I am."

"But it's different now!" she said angrily. "Fred, don't you realize what you've done? You've shot an innocent man."

"Only to keep him from shooting me."

Fiercely, she said, "I wish he had! If you were dead, it'd all be over."

I got up and poured myself another drink. "Well, if that's how you feel, you can still sic the cops on me yourself."

She stared at the blank tube of the big color TV and shook her head. "No," she whispered. "I don't know why, Fred, but in spite of everything that's happened, I still love you. That's what's so terrible."

I sat down and patted her knee. "It gives me pleasure to hear you say that. Big woman, I just couldn't believe things was so bad that they'd ruin everything we had between us."

She stroked my hair. "But don't you see that I can't let you go on with this stupid killing?" She stopped. "No, I guess you don't. Words just don't get across to you, do they?"

"Hush up," I said. "I thought we wasn't going to argue anymore."

She pressed my hand against her mouth. "I *had* to be there in the park. I *had* to get mixed up with you. If only we could go back and do everything all over again."

"Well," I said, "like I always say——"

"I know," she said. "You get no guarantee on tomorrow."

She hugged my neck, so I picked her up and took her
to bed, and it was the best yet.

Only I woke up this morning, and she had gone, and
took all her clothes and my rifle with her.

NINETEEN

Sid Michaelson leaned back in his chair. It wasn't hot, but he was sweating.

"That happened this morning?"

"Just like I said. So I called you."

"Why?"

"Well, maybe Alice changed her mind. Maybe she's going to sic The Law on me after all. Maybe she's decided to come after me like all the rest."

Sid looked at his watch. "It's been hours. If she'd turned you in, they'd be here by now."

"I reckon you're right. I guess I don't really believe that's what she'd do. She despised that jailhouse so much, I don't think she could bear to put me in there, no matter how much she hates what I did."

Angrily, he said, "And what do you expect me to do?"

"Well, you're my lawyer. I want you to help me."

"Fred, for God's sake! If you've done what you've

told me you have, do you think I'd lift a finger to keep you out of the electric chair?"

"Why not?"

He cursed and ground his cigar out on the rug. It made a big black burn mark.

"All right," he said, "you listen good. I'm not involved with you in this in any way, do you understand? You haven't convinced me that you killed all those people, you haven't convinced me of even *one*. There's no trace of a gun or ammunition either in this apartment, and no evidence that they've ever been here. There's not even any evidence that Alice has been here since I got her out of jail. Now, I have a future in politics. Ten years from now, I may even run for mayor of this city. If you think I'm going to let you tar my name with this insanity, you're even crazier than Alice said you were."

"But I told you the truth."

He got up. "Not the way I see it. As far as I'm concerned, you're just another one of the crackpots who come out of the woodwork after every well-publicized crime and claim all the credit. Some of them are very convincing, but you aren't, old man. All you want is a little attention."

"All I want is to get out of this with my hide. If Alice has gone sour, she could hurt me."

"I don't think you've got a thing to worry about," he said. "Why don't you just go back to Kansas and forget the whole thing? I will."

"I might just do that. But what about this lousy city. Do you think the folks here'll forget what happened?"

"That's none of your business, is it? It's only your own hide you're worried about, isn't that what you said? Well, get on a bus and clear out. A little of you goes a long way, Fred. I think we've had a sufficient dose."

"I reckon that's what I'll do," I said. "There's sure enough a sour taste to everything around here now. What with Alice taking off like that, and you bad-mouthing me. I thought you were my friend."

"Just do me one favor," he said. "Forget you ever heard my name. And don't stop riding until you cross the Mississippi."

He even slammed the door on his way out.

How about that? Who can you figure? Who can you trust?

I stuck my money in a small suitcase along with some clothes. I didn't feel like hauling much. Those fancy suits would be out of place in the high country, anyway.

For once, the elevator came quickly. There was a second, as the door first opened, when I almost expected to find Mary Lou in it.

But there were only shadows.

Bernie was mopping the lobby.

"Going on a trip, Fred?"

"What's it look like?"

"Alice going with you?"

"Any business of yours?"

He got a hurt expression. "I'm sorry, Fred. It's just that when she left this morning, she told me to tell you that she'd catch up with you."

237

I looked at him. "Is that exactly what she said?"

He shrugged. "More or less. She said that you shouldn't worry, that she'd make sure everything was all right. I think she said something like she'd be sure to come after you."

I tightened my hand on the suitcase. "Well, if you see her, Bernie, you tell her——"

"Tell her what?"

I started for the sidewalk. "Nothing. I guess it's too late for talking."

TWENTY

Winter was sneaking into town. The north wind nibbled around my ankles and scattered old newspapers down the sidewalk.

There weren't any cabs in sight. The chilly streets were deserted. My footsteps echoed off the dingy buildings as I started for the subway.

Behind me, up on one of the roofs, I heard the metallic click of a rifle bolt.